AN OFFER HE CAN'T REFUSE

"You're my very best friend and I don't want anything to change that."

"I don't want anything to change our friendship, either." Reaching across the table, Ric took her hand and smiled at her.

"Good, good." Anna May took a deep breath and gathered her courage. "You know I'd never ask you for something unless I really, really needed it. I mean unless it's a birthday present or something, but you know, I don't really ask for anything. We've been friends for a long time, and I care about you," she said hurriedly, ending on a breathless note.

Ric stared at her with a puzzled look on his face. "Are you nervous? You're talking a mile a minute." He squeezed her hand to reassure her. "Anything I have is yours for the asking, Anna May. Anything. What do you need? I'll get it for you."

She closed her eyes and fought the fear which had her heart beating wildly. "Ric, will you marry me and be the father of my child?"

She watched as shock, disbelief, then rage appeared on his face. "Pregnant?"

Shaking her head, Anna May replied, "No, no. I'm not pregnant. I want you to get me pregnant."

IF ONLY
YOU KNEW

Carla Fredd

Pinnacle Books
Kensington Publishing Corp.

PINNACLE BOOKS are published by

Kensington Publishing Corp.
850 Third Avenue
New York, NY 10022

Pinnacle, the P logo, and Arabesque are Reg. U.S. Pat. & TM Off.

First Printing: October, 1996

Printed in the United States of America
10 9 8 7 6 5 4 3 2 1

This book is dedicated to
my heroes
Gary W. Levister, who would, and to J. Darrin Evans,
who wouldn't.
Thanks, guys.

Prologue

"I'll be good, Mama. I'll be good." Six-year-old Ric Justice cried as his mother walked to the door of his grandmother's small shotgun home. His mother had opened the windows when they arrived, and now the smell of pinto beans from the stove clashed with her perfume and hot stifling summer heat.

"I can't take you back with me. You know Evan doesn't like it when you touch his things, and you went into his desk and wrote on his important papers." She rocked her youngest son, Adam, in her arms when he began to fret.

"I won't do it again," Ric replied as he wiped the tears from his eyes. "I want to go home with you and Adam."

"Take him with you. Why should I be saddled with him?" came a voice from behind Ric. "I told you not to marry that no-good soldier in the first place, and what do you have to show for it? A dead soldier's child to take care of. I don't blame Evan for not wanting the child in his house when he has his own child to feed.''

"Mama, Ric won't be any trouble. Will you?" she said with a smile.

"I want to go with you," Ric said.

"You can't, honey." She picked up the baby bag and placed it over her arm. "Now give Mama a kiss."

Ric walked across the room and kissed his mother's cheek. He was careful not to mess up her makeup. Mama didn't like it when he messed up her makeup.

"I love you, sugarplum," she said carelessly. "Now stay with Grandma and be a good boy."

"You're not giving me enough money to take care of the kid. How am I supposed to eat and feed him, too?"

"Evan's taking care of that, Mama. Bye, Ric. Say goodbye to Adam," she said turning the baby so that the two brothers faced each other.

"Bye, Adam," Ric said, and the tears began to fall again. His chest hurt, and he felt as if he couldn't breathe. "Maaamaaa."

"Hush now, Ric, and be a good boy." She smiled and walked out of the door.

Ric hung his head and cried.

The blow was hard and fast but not unexpected. Ric rubbed his leg, trying to ease the stinging pain. "Hush before I give you something to cry about."

Ric tried to be quiet, but he couldn't control the whimpers that escaped.

"Hush, boy," his grandmother yelled and delivered another blow to his leg. "You'd better mind me. Your mama doesn't want you with her, and if you don't mind me, you'll be put in a home and nobody will want you then.''

Ric cried silently as his grandmother left the room. He had to be good. Maybe if he was good enough, then his mother would come back for him.

Chapter One

She wasn't going to make it home.

Anna May Robinson gripped the steering wheel tighter as a blast of arctic wind coated the windshield with sleet and ice, blowing her Galant into the next lane of the nearly deserted highway. Normally on a Friday night, traffic would be heavy with weary travelers leaving Atlanta's busy international airport. She'd traveled down this highway many times over the last few months. For the first time tonight, she felt a twinge of fear. She could barely see the red taillights of a car in front of her, and she hadn't seen any signs of a car behind her in the last thirty minutes.

As she passed a line of abandoned cars on the side of the road, she wondered if she should pull over and wait out the storm. The shrill, howling sound of the wind convinced her to keep driving.

According to the radio announcer, she was in the middle of one of the worst ice storms in Atlanta's history. From the time she'd merged onto I-285 an hour ago, she'd watched snow cover the tall pine trees that lined the highway, creating a beautiful winter wonderland. But as the sunlight began to fade, snow became ice. Young trees snapped like matchsticks, and old trees were doubled over under the weight of the ice.

With each pass of the windshield wipers, she said a prayer. She prayed for herself and the other poor souls who were out in the storm tonight.

Maybe I should have stayed in the airport or tried to get a hotel room, she thought. She grimaced with distaste at the thought of spending another night in a hotel room. For the past three weeks, she'd stayed in a hotel. She and four of her co-workers in the public relations department handled the press releases announcing her company's buyout of their major competitor to major newspapers, magazines, and television. She was sick of hotels. She wanted to sleep in her own bed and cook her own food, but it seemed the only place she'd be sleeping tonight would be in her car.

Without warning, she drove over a patch of black ice, sending her car skidding across the highway. "Keep calm, keep calm," she said. Her words were contradictory to the icy waves of fear that spread throughout her body. Anna May turned in the direction of the skid and took her foot off the gas pedal. Her hands shook as she brought the car under control.

She wasn't going to make it if the road was like this all the way to her house in Decatur. She was going to have to find a place to stay tonight or until the storm was over. If she hadn't exchanged tickets with her co-worker, she wouldn't be in this mess. But Cally, her co-worker, had a husband and a seven-month-old son that she hadn't seen in three weeks. There was no one at home waiting for her. Despite the awful weather, Anna May would have done the same thing.

The wind whirled around her, making it difficult for her to keep the car steady. Her shoulders began to burn with fatigue from leaning forward to get a better view of the highway. Snow swirled wildly around the dimly lit green sign. I-675. One mile. The exit to Ric's house. Her salvation.

Ric Justice was the love of her life. The only man she'd ever loved. She'd been fourteen years old when he'd moved in across the street.

Anna May smiled as she remembered the first time she saw him. He was every teenage girl's dream dressed in gym shorts that hot summer afternoon. His T-shirt thrown on the sidewalk in front of his aunt's house. Sweat gleamed on his copper brown chest and shoulders. The late afternoon sun brought out red highlights in his dark brown hair.

She supposed what she felt when she saw him was what her Sunday school teacher called lust of the flesh. At the time, Sunday school was the last thing on her mind. He moved with grace as he pushed the lawn mower across the lawn. She'd waited until he finished mowing the lawn before she walked across the street. His cool response to her didn't stop her from being friendly to him. In fact, his response made her more determined to be his friend. Over the next nineteen years, her lust and friendship had developed into love . . . love that Ric didn't return.

She punched a button on her car phone and gave a verbal command to dial Ric's number.

"Justice." His voice was deep and smooth like honey.

"Ric, it's Anna May."

"Where are you? You sound like you're on a car phone."

"I am. I just got back in town. The roads are too icy for me to get to my house. I'm about a mile away from your exit."

"You left the airport in this mess?"

Anna May winced. Although he hadn't raised his voice, Ric's quiet tone communicated his displeasure with the skill and precision of a seasoned marksman.

As much as she loved Ric, she did not intend to let him talk down to her. "It wasn't like this when I left an hour ago, *Garrick*. I'm not crazy enough to start driving home in an ice storm."

"The weather turned dangerous about thirty minutes ago. Why didn't you stop then?"

"I thought I could make it home," Anna May replied.

"No, you were too stubborn to admit defeat."

"Don't get smart with me, Ric." The wind howled. Its force battered her car as if to push it across the deserted highway. She tightened her grip on the steering wheel to keep her car under control.

"What the hell is that noise?"

"The wind. I'm scared, Ric."

"Pull over on the side of the road, and I'll come and get you."

"No. Both of us don't need to be out in this mess. I'll call you if I run into any trouble."

"Don't you hang up, Anna May. You stay on the line until you get to my house." The tone of his voice conveyed a message of: Do what I say and I mean it. She knew he was worried. He'd only use that stern tone of voice when he was worried.

She could almost picture him pacing back and

forth, with his dark brown eyebrows drawn together in a frown. His head lowered as if contemplating the best way to get her to his home.

"I can't concentrate on driving and talk to you at the same time," she said.

"We don't have to talk. I just need to know that you aren't having trouble out there," he said.

Her heart melted. Ric wasn't one to show his feelings, but when he said things like that to her, she knew he really cared about her. "All right, I'll stay on the line."

Forty-five minutes later, she breathed a sigh of relief when she reached the private road that led to Ric's house.

"I made it," she whispered.

"Did you say something, Anna May?"

"Yes, I just reached your road. I'm almost there."

Thick groves of pecan trees lined either side of the road. She drove at a snail's pace, going around fallen limbs when she could and driving over them when she couldn't. Finally, she inched around the last curve in the road. Ric's one-hundred-year-old, three-story farmhouse was ablaze with lights.

Then she saw him.

Ric stood staring out of the large picture window, holding a cordless telephone to his ear, watching and waiting for her. "Park in the garage," he said and hung up the phone. The four-car garage was a separate building joined to the house by an enclosed breezeway. It was the only addition he'd made when he bought the house. A single garage door was open. She drove inside and parked her car. She laid her head on the steering wheel. The tense muscles in her shoulders protested against her movement. The slight pain was inconsequential to the relief she felt now that the ordeal of driving on ice was over.

She lifted her head at the sound of tapping on the driver-side window.

"Are you all right?" he asked as he leaned down beside her car. His voice was forceful and shadowed with worry.

He looked every inch a successful businessman. His crisp, white shirt fit his broad shoulders like a glove. His subdued paisley tie was firmly in place. Most people would have changed into casual clothes when they came home, but Ric never changed if he planned to work at home. It was only when he turned off his laptop that he changed into casual clothing.

"Anna May," he said in a tone that demanded her attention.

She met his golden brown gaze and was floored by the unmistakable masculine beauty of him. Over the years she'd developed an art of hiding her feelings for him behind a mask of friendship. But it took time to put that mask in place, time that she hadn't had. Lord, she loved this man.

Get your act together, she thought to herself and pasted a friendly smile on her face. "I'm fine," she said.

She picked up her purse from the passenger seat and stepped out of the car.

He was big. She'd always felt diminutive standing next to his six-foot six-inch frame. Ric grasped her shoulders as if to make sure she was really there. The subtle fragrance of his cologne enveloped her senses. Then he smiled at her. His deep masculine dimples appeared. What she would give to have him smile at her the way her father smiled at her mother, with love. A blast of cold air brought her back to reality.

"Come on, let's get you inside," he said. "Do you need anything out of the car?"

"Just my suitcase." She walked to the back of the car and opened the trunk. Ric reached inside and removed the bag. When he closed the trunk, she wondered if she'd made the right choice. If she didn't put some distance between them, she was afraid that she'd do something to drive away her very best friend in the world. She couldn't bear the thought of that happening.

Anna May felt refreshed after the hot shower. The red sweat suit and sneakers were more her rather than the business suit she'd worn earlier. I'm glad I carried it with me on this trip, she thought. Making her way downstairs, thick carpet muffling the sound of her footsteps, she searched for Ric. She found him in the kitchen. Leaning against the doorway, she watched him carefully pour hot water into a cup. His movements were precise and controlled, much like the man himself. Even his house had a sense of exacting order about it—from the braided throw rug in the foyer to the ceramic canisters in the kitchen— everything in the house was neat and in place. Everything was also very boring.

"You know it wouldn't hurt if you put plants in the window," she said as she walked to the window above the sink. "A cactus would thrive in this window, and it doesn't require any work on your part."

Ric tilted his head to the side as if visualizing cacti in the window. "No. I like it like it is."

"Boorrring," she said as she rolled her eyes.

"Just because your house resembles the Amazon

rain forest doesn't mean that I want mine to look
like a jungle.''

"One plant does not make a jungle."

"If I thought you'd be content with just one plant,
I'd get one—but before I knew it you'd have a plant
in every room in the house." He placed the tea bag
in a cup.

"That's not exactly true," she said watching him
lift then lower the tea bag into the cup.

Ric smiled. "Then why do I have dried flowers all
over my house?"

"It's potpourri. You said you liked it."

"Yes, I liked it in the den," he said turning his
attention away from the cup of tea to look at her.

"What's the use of having it just in the den?"

Ric laughed and shook his head. "Never mind,
Anna May. Here's your decaffeinated tea. I'm surprised you're drinking anything decaffeinated," he
said as he gave her the cup.

"I'm cutting out caffeine in my diet."

"What brought that on? I've been on your case for
years to cut down on caffeine."

She took a sip of tea then said, "I'm following my
doctor's advice."

"There's nothing wrong, is there?" A thin line
formed between his brows.

Her stomach growled, reminding her that she
hadn't eaten since lunch. "Nothing that a good dinner won't take care of. Speaking of dinner, what's
there to eat around here?" She turned away from
him, evading his questioning gaze and opened a cabinet.

"Here," he said opening a drawer. "Have some of
these."

"These" were a miniature box of lemon drop

candy. Her favorite. He always had the candy in his home. It was one of the small things he did to show that he cared for her.

Anna May held out her hand and smiled as he carefully shook two pieces of candy, her normal limit, into her palm. "Mmm. Thanks."

"You're welcome," he replied tossing the empty box into the trash then going to the refrigerator. "How about steak for dinner? It's already thawed."

"Sounds good," she said and placed her cup on the counter.

Together they prepared steaks, baked sweet potatoes, and tossed salad. They sat at the breakfast bar eating their dinner and listening to the weather report on the radio.

"Looks like we'll be snowed in for a few days," Ric said when the report ended.

"Yeah," she said. A few days alone with Ric. It would be heaven. It would be hell. Could she keep her feelings for him hidden? She didn't want to think about it.

"So how did you get stuck in this weather?" he asked. "I thought you said you had an earlier flight."

"I did but I switched with Cally. She hasn't seen her little boy in three weeks, and it didn't seem fair for her to sit in the airport for another two hours when she could be with her baby."

He shook his head. "Anna May, you're always taking care of everybody else. When are you going to take care of you?"

She sighed. They'd had this discussion before, and no matter how many times she tried to explain herself, Ric never understood her need to give to others. "I *do* take care of me. Switching flights with Cally wasn't a big deal. I like helping others. I like making people happy," she said shrugging her shoulders. "There's no harm in that."

He raised his brows. "No harm," he said sarcastically. "You could have been stuck in your car and froze to death. You could have had an accident. Anything could have happened to you as a result of switching to a later flight."

"How was I supposed to know there was going to be an ice storm?"

"If you knew, would you have given up your flight?" he asked as he cut his steak.

She grimaced with guilt. He knew her too well. "I uhmm . . ."

"You'd have given up your seat anyway. Wouldn't you?" he asked quietly—however his frustration came through loud and clear.

She nodded yes then said, "But her son is only a few months old and she hasn't seen him in so long."

Ric shook his head and his brown eyes gleamed with determination. "You've been away from home for the same amount of time. You needed to come home just as much as your co-worker."

Placing her hand over her heart, she replied, "I don't have a family waiting for me at home like Cally does."

"True, but you do have family and *friends* that want you to get home in one piece."

"Speaking of which," she said as she stood, "I'd better check the messages on my answering machine. If my parents or either of my brothers heard about this storm, they'll have been calling to see if I made it home."

She had six messages on her machine. Her parents had called twice, both of her brothers, her best friend, Janet, and Cally had left messages to call as soon as she got home. She called her family, reassuring each of them that she was safe and sound at Ric's house. Her brothers gave her grief about driving in the storm, and no amount of explaining would convince them that it was not her fault that she was caught by surprise in the storm. When she finally got off the phone, she wished that she was an only child.

"Would you like to have two older brothers? They're free," she said leaning against the kitchen wall.

"No, thanks. I don't need any more family."

She winced at his harsh, unyielding tone. "I was just kidding, Ric."

"I wasn't." He cleared the dishes off of the table and began to load them in the dishwasher.

Family had always been a touchy subject with Ric. She knew that he and his aunt and uncle weren't close and couldn't understand why. The Stewards were hard-working, kind people. Anna May had witnessed Ric's rejection of their affection several times when they were still in high school. When she'd asked him why he acted the way he did, he'd either change the subject, or if she pressed him for an answer, Ric would tell her in no uncertain terms that he didn't want to talk about it.

For the most part she'd avoided the subject of family when she was with him, but sometimes she would forget to be careful. Family was such a large part of her life. She couldn't imagine not having a close, loving relationship with her family.

"I've got to call Janet," she said when he continued to stack the dishes.

Next to Ric, Janet Hill was her closest friend. They'd met in college and been friends ever since. For all of the bad-girl front that Janet portrayed, she was a caring, tenderhearted person. The phone rang only once before Janet answered.

"Hi, Janet."

"Where the *hell* are you?" she demanded. "It's nine o'clock. You said your flight was due in at five o'clock. I've been calling your house every hour on the hour for the past two hours. I finally tried your car phone and got no answer—"

"I'm at Ric's," Anna May interrupted.

There was silence on the other end of the line. "You're at Ric's? Alone? Just the two of you?"

"Yes," Anna May said as Ric placed the last dish in the dishwasher and left the room.

"Good. Maybe Ric will realize that it's you that he loves, and ya'll will make mad passionate love."

"Hah. Fat chance." Anna May couldn't keep the hurt from sounding in her voice.

"Sometimes you just have to take a chance, Anna May."

"Taking chances is your job. You're the stock-broker."

"Stocks, bonds, and annuities aren't the same as a loving man."

"I know. I'm glad you aren't out in the storm. Do you have enough food.?"

"Changing the subject, are we?" Janet asked drolly. "I'll let it go for now."

Anna May talked to Janet for a few minutes more before going in search of Ric.

She found him in the den, her favorite room in the house. A large stone fireplace with gas logs dominated the room. Ornate crown molding decorated the fifteen-foot-high walls. Four nine-foot windows lined the wall opposite the fireplace. The room reflected Ric's need for order. This room, like the kitchen, had everything in place. It looked like a showroom model of what a den should be. The room was beautiful, but it needed something to make it come alive.

Ric sat in a large leather chair that she privately called his throne. He looked up from the book he was reading when she walked into the room.

"Did you get in touch with Janet?"

"Yes." She sat on the navy blue sleeper sofa and propped her feet on the coffee table.

Ric stared at her sock-clad feet. "Did you know you have a hole in your sock?"

"Yep." She wiggled her toes. When he continued to stare at the hole, she put her foot across her knee. "If that hole bothers you, I can turn it around so it faces me."

He gave her an annoyed look.

"What are you reading?" she asked.

"A book."

Anna May grabbed one of the pillows scattered on the sofa and threw it at him. He caught the pillow and set it aside.

"Testy, testy," he said then smiled.

"Just answer the question, smart-mouth," she said.

"Silence of the Lambs."

"Oh," she muttered. "Have you gotten to the part where—"

"Anna May, don't do it."

"Do what?"

"Tell me about the book." He glared at her then closed the book.

"Don't stop reading on my account. I promise not to tell you how the book ended."

She looked around the room, hoping that something other than Ric would catch her attention. Her gaze returned to Ric.

"Where are the cards?"

Ric nodded to the entertainment center next to the fireplace. "Look on the bottom shelf."

She went to the entertainment center. Cassette tapes and CD's were neatly stacked on the shelf. She found the pack of cards resting on top of a checkerboard set. She picked up both items and returned to her place on the sofa. She spread the cards on the coffee table and began to play.

"What are you doing?" he asked.

"Playing solitaire," she replied meeting his puzzled gaze.

"You don't have to do that. I'll play a game with you."

"No, read your book. I'm fine," Anna May said as she placed a card on top of another.

"Are you sure?"

"I'm sure."

Ric shrugged his shoulders then opened the book and began to read. She let her gaze linger over his strong face His features were as familiar to her as her own. His high forehead had a tiny scar above his right eyebrow—a football injury. She'd been there when he was tackled and hit his head. She'd screamed when she'd seen the amount of blood streaming down his face. Ric still teased her about the blood-curdling scream, as he called it. Anna May smiled at the memory then placed another card on the table.

She needed to wind down without imposing on Ric. She'd seen the flash of longing when he'd closed the book. If she asked, he would join her in a game of cards, but Ric rarely had the time to read for pleasure these days, and she didn't want to intrude on his time.

After several boring hands of solitaire, Anna May had had enough.

"Don't you want to do something?" she asked in desperation.

Ric never stopped reading his book. "I am doing something."

"I mean, don't you want to do something together?"

"You're bored, aren't you?"

"Kinda. Sorta."

He marked his place in the book before he closed it and set it on the table beside him. "Okay, what do you want to do?"

One hour later Anna May stared at the checkers on the board. Ric had her cornered. No matter what move she made, she was going to lose . . . for the third time.

"You're going to have to make a move sooner or later," he said, his voice tinged with regret.

"I know," she said making no attempt to move the game forward. She looked up from the board and saw the hint of a smile on Ric's face. "I don't have any hope of winning this game, do I?"

"No."

The lights flickered then went out completely. The light from the fireplace cast a faint orange glow about the room.

"Does this mean I win the game by default?" Anna May asked.

His rich laughter filled the darkened room. "No. Stay here while I get a flashlight and some candles."

He entered the room a few minutes later and closed the door behind him. "It's going to get pretty cold in the rest of the house if the electricity doesn't come on soon." He set a portable radio, a flashlight, a box of candles, and a book of matches on the coffee table. "The gas logs will keep this room warm if we stay in here."

Anna May tried to stifle a yawn but couldn't. The events of the day had finally taken a toll on her. "Sorry, I just realized how tired I am."

"That's okay. I'll go upstairs and get some extra blankets. You can sleep on the sofa bed, and I'll sleep on the floor."

"Oh, Ric—you don't have to sleep on the cold floor."

"The carpet is thick, and I'll be closer to the fireplace than you will so I won't be cold."

"But—"

"I'm sleeping on the floor, Anna May."

She recognized the stubborn tone in his voice. He wasn't going to change his mind no matter what she said.

"Okay. I'll follow you upstairs. I need my suitcase."

Ric led the way upstairs. He gave her the flashlight when they reached the guest room. "I've got another flashlight in my bedroom," he said when she gave him a puzzled look.

The guest bedroom had a private bathroom. While brushing her teeth, she debated whether or not to change into her pajamas. She decided against the pajamas. She'd need the warmth of her sweat suit if the electricity didn't come on.

Who would have thought that she'd be spending the night in the same room with Ric. She'd laugh if the situation weren't so pitiful.

She put the toothbrush in her toilet kit. From the bottom of the bag, she removed a bottle of iron pills that her doctor prescribed. She swallowed the pill and took a sip of water. For the past month taking an iron pill had become a part of her nightly routine. If she could go through with the rest of her doctor's advice, she would be fine.

Anna May reached inside the bag again and removed a small jewelry box. She laid the top on the counter and lifted a gold ring suspended from a chain. Ric had given her the ring years ago. She slipped the chain around her neck and tucked the ring beneath her sweatshirt. Only once had she not slept with the ring between her breasts, and that was when she'd had surgery a few years ago.

"Anna May," Ric called through the door. "I'm going downstairs. Do you want me to wait for you?"

Anna May touched the ring beneath her shirt, closed her bag, and walked to the door. "I'll go with you."

He'd changed into khaki pants and a plaid flannel shirt. Both items were pressed and starched.

They carried pillows and blankets that would become Ric's bed downstairs to the den. Ric moved the coffee table and unfolded the sofa bed. Each of them prepared their own bed. Anna May laid in the bed, and watched him lay the final blanket on the floor.

"Good night, Ric."

"Good night, Anna May." He blew out the candle.

She heard the rustle of covers when he laid down. A few minutes later, she heard his restless movements. She opened her eyes and saw him take off his shirt. His tight muscles seemed to glow in the firelight as he folded his shirt and laid it on the floor. Anna May closed her eyes. Suddenly she wasn't tired.

* * *

She didn't know what awakened her later that night. It could have been the sound of the door opening or the cool air that flowed into the room from the open door. She sat up, brushing her hair off her face. Rumpled blankets marked the spot where Ric once lay.

"Did I wake you up?" Ric walked into the room carrying a cup and a flashlight. Sometime during the night, he'd put on his shirt.

"Hmm. What are you drinking?" she asked, her voice husky from sleep.

"Tea."

"Couldn't you sleep?" she asked as the minty fragrance of tea reached her.

"I'll go to sleep once I finish this." He put the flashlight on the coffee table, then he lowered himself to the floor.

"Good night," she said lying back in the bed. She watched him hold the cup of tea with both hands then take a sip. The flannel shirt stretched tightly across his shoulders. He seemed to be mesmerized by the flames in the fireplace. That's when she saw him shiver. She threw the covers off the bed and walked over to him.

He looked up in surprise. "What are you doing?"

She placed the back of her hand against his cheek. He was ice cold.

"Were you going to spend all night freezing on the floor?" She didn't wait for him to answer. Pointing to the sofa bed, she said, "Get in that bed."

"I'll be fine. I just need to warm up a little," he insisted.

"If you're worried about your virtue, I'll stay on

my side of the bed and you can stay on yours. But you can best believe that both of us will be in that bed or"—she paused—"both of us will be freezing on the floor. What do you want to do?"

Ric leisurely drank the last of his hot tea until she sat down beside him in front of the fireplace.

He glared at her.

Anna May smiled at him.

Ric set his cup on the table then stood to his feet.

"Come on," he said holding out his hand.

Anna May took his hand and stood. Together they walked to the sofa bed.

As she lay down on her side of the bed, she wondered if she'd ever fall asleep. She and Ric were in bed together. It was an event she was sure would never happen.

"Good night," Ric said then settled in the bed with his back toward her.

"Night, Ric," she replied. *There's no way I'm going to fall asleep. No way.* She turned on her side with her back to him, pulled the covers over her shoulders, and stared into the darkness. *It was going to be a long night,* she thought.

Chapter Two

The early Saturday morning sun peeked through the windows in the den. Anna May opened her eyes and stretched her arms. The arm draped over her waist tightened. She froze in midstretch. Ric snuggled next to her in spoonlike fashion. Even through the fabric of her sweat suit, she could feel his arousal against her hip.

"Good Lord," she whispered, heat rushing to her face. How was she going to get out of the bed without awakening him? If he woke up now, they would both be embarrassed. Maybe she should lie there pretending to be asleep until he woke up. That wouldn't work. She had to go to the bathroom. Soon. She carefully took his arm and tried to move out of his embrace. Instead of releasing her, Ric moved even closer to her. If she wanted to get out of the bed, she'd have to wake him. She took a deep breath and shook his arm.

* * *

He was hard as a rock, and it was all because of Anna May Robinson. The tile felt cool beneath his hands as he braced himself against the bathroom wall. A forceful spray of cold water streamed down his chest and legs, doing little to improve his condition. For months he'd kept his attraction to Anna May under control, hiding it behind the shield of friendship. In one night he'd blown his control totally.

He knew the exact moment that his feelings for her had changed. Last summer she'd convinced him to attend a cookout given by her next-door neighbors. In a business setting, he could socialize with anyone; however, when it came to personal environments, he tended to stay to himself. He would have done the same thing at the cookout, but Anna May wouldn't let him. She introduced him to her neighbors, a young couple recently married. Before he knew it, he was mingling with the other guests, discussing everything from the national news to the chances of the Atlanta Braves winning the World Series while eating hot dogs and potato salad. He, along with some of the other men, set up a volleyball net.

The guests divided into teams and positioned themselves on the freshly cut grass. He and Anna May played on the same team. With the game tied, they both attempted to hit the ball over the net. They collided, throwing them both off balance. He landed on his back, and air rushed out of his lungs when Anna May landed on top of him. It hadn't occurred to him that his best friend was a woman until her long legs tangled with his, and her soft breasts were pressed against his chest. Desire rushed hot and wild through his body, intensifying when her hips brushed against his manhood. He would have kissed her sense-

less then and there if she hadn't quickly gotten to
her feet with the help of one of the team members.

The other guests must have thought him strange.
He was quiet the rest of the party, trying to come to
grips with his attraction to Anna May. It was as if he
saw her for the very first time and he couldn't get
enough of the sight of her. The green cotton T-shirt
clung to her breasts. White walking shorts accented
her shapely hips. He found himself watching her every
move the rest of the afternoon until he couldn't bear
to watch her without doing something about it. That's
exactly what he'd done, nothing. He wasn't about to
ruin his friendship with her because his hormones
had kicked into overdrive. Besides, Anna May was the
kind of woman who believed in the happily ever after.
She wanted a husband, two children, and a house in
the suburbs. She wanted a family . . . something he
wouldn't give her.

With a savage twist, he turned off the shower and
brushed aside the past memories. He grabbed a towel,
wrapped it around his waist, and walked into the
bedroom.

"I should have never agreed to get into the bed
with her in the first place," he muttered. His body
had betrayed him while he slept. Now the damage
was done. Anna May was innocent in many ways, but
there was no denying the physical evidence that he
wanted her. He couldn't lie to himself and excuse
his arousal as one of those early morning things that
happened. He'd been dreaming of the two of them
making love. It was Anna May who he wanted.

Just thinking about the way her body fit perfectly
against his was enough to destroy what little relief
the cold shower had provided. Last night the layer
of clothing that had separated them seemed nonexis-

tent. He could still feel the firm, subtle curve of her hips nestled against his manhood, the weight of her breasts against his forearm, and the chain with the ring he'd given her warm with the heat of her body. The ring was an IOU, and each time he saw it, which was almost every time he saw her, it reminded him of the debt he owed. A debt he had yet to repay.

He had to get himself under control, he thought. As much as he wanted Anna May physically, he wanted . . . no, he needed her friendship more. He knew from experience that the emotion called love between a man and a woman didn't last. His brief engagement to Lena had shown him that.

Anna May had been his friend for almost twenty years. He hoped that this wouldn't destroy their relationship. He tried to imagine what his life would be like without her off beat sense of humor and her damn-the-torpedoes, full-steam-ahead view of the world. No, he thought, his jaw tightened with determination, he wouldn't let last night change their friendship. He'd do whatever it took to keep Anna May in his life as his friend.

Ric dressed slowly despite the frigid temperature of the room. Running his multi-million-dollar company required planning. Facing Anna May after last night also required a plan. He just had to think of one.

Anna May straightened the sheets and folded the sofa bed into place. Within minutes all traces of last night's activities were gone, but not forgotten. She doubted that she would ever forget the feel of his body curled around hers or the soft stroke of his fingers gliding beneath her sweatshirt, cupping her breasts. She shivered as she remembered the husky sound of his voice as he whispered "Anna." Ric Justice had wanted her!

She was happy. She was terrified. For once in her life, she wished that she had more experience with men. Her friends thought she should have been born a century ago because she was still a virgin at the age of thirty-three. Being the only daughter of a minister, she'd made up her mind years ago to wait until she was married before becoming intimate with anyone. She'd never regretted her decision.

Her thoughts were interrupted by the sudden absence of sound. She realized that Ric had finished his shower. Soon he would come downstairs.

How would he treat her? How would she respond? Would she have the courage to put their friendship on the line and ask him to marry her and more importantly give her a child?

If her friends or family knew what she was planning, they would be shocked.

Her dream of marrying and having children all but died when her doctor informed her of her test results. She had to choose between never having a child of her own or having a child now while she still could. She'd thought long and hard about having a child after that visit to the doctor. It was now time for her to make a choice. Her choice was to have a child. Ric's child.

She hadn't planned to ask him so soon. When she'd made up her mind to ask Ric to marry her and father her child, she'd envisioned having him over for dinner and talking it over with him. Like she'd discussed her decision to stay in Atlanta when the rest of her family moved to California ten years ago or when she thought of buying a house a few years back. Most of the major decisions she'd made in her life, she had asked his opinion on the subject first. She hadn't always agreed with his opinion. In the end she'd made her own decision, but it was nice to have him to talk to as a friend.

The risk she was about to take was high. She knew how Ric felt about family. She knew it and didn't understand it. Her greatest fear was that Ric would turn her down and end their friendship. She hoped and prayed that it would never happen, but she couldn't go through life knowing she hadn't tried to have a child.

Her stomach growled, reminding her that it was time to eat breakfast. Anna May left the den and entered the kitchen. The view from the large window was daunting. The sun was hidden behind gray clouds heavy with sleet and frozen rain. During the night the weather conditions had worsened. Every surface was covered with a thick layer of ice, and icicles hung from the eaves of the roof. I won't be going home today, she thought to herself. She was stuck in the house with Ric for at least another day.

"It looks like it's going to snow again."

She jumped at the sound of his voice, pausing briefly to compose herself, then turned to him. He'd changed into black baggy pants, a black cotton sweater with a black turtleneck, and black hiking boots. Any other man would have looked casual and relaxed. Ric looked in command, in control.

"Yes, it does." She looked at his face, searching for any sign of what he might be feeling, but he kept his emotions hidden behind what she called his stone face—an expression that he used when he was nervous. Ignoring her own nervousness, she removed a glass from the cabinet and filled it with water from the sink. An uneasy silence filled the room. She took a sip of water then set the glass on the counter. "So what's for breakfast?"

He opened the refrigerator door. "Bacon, eggs, biscuits, orange juice?"

"What about grits?"

"The box is in the cabinet."

Ric set the table while Anna May prepared breakfast on the gas stove. She was as familiar with his kitchen as she was her own, but even in the familiar setting, she felt uneasy. She wanted to break the tension between them but didn't know how. Several times she started to speak to him, but she couldn't think of anything to say. She set platters of food on the table then sat down to eat.

They ate in silence. Halfway through the meal, she put down her fork.

"Ric," she said hesitantly. "About what happened on the sofa . . ."

He put down his fork and leaned back in his chair. "Anna May, I'm sorry about that . . ."

"No. Let me finish, or I'll never have the courage to do this again," she said. She met his eyes for a brief second before looking down at her plate. "On the sofa you were—what I'm trying to say is you were physically attracted to me, weren't you?"

"Yes, but—" he said reluctantly.

She interrupted. "And now you're wondering how I'm going to react. In all the years we've known each other, this has never happened before." She looked at him. "You're still my very best friend, and I don't want anything to change that," she said in a rush.

"I don't want anything to change our friendship either." Reaching across the table, he took her hand and smiled at her. Long masculine dimples appeared in his cheeks.

Anna May squeezed his hand and placed her other hand on top of his. "Good." She took a deep breath and gathered her courage. "You know I'd never ask you for something unless I really, really needed it. I mean unless it's a birthday present or something I don't usually ask for anything. We've been friends for a long time, and I care about you," she said hurriedly, ending on a breathless note.

He stared at her with a puzzled look on his face. "Are you nervous? You're talking a mile a minute." He squeezed her hand as if to reassure her. "Anything I have is yours for the asking, Anna May. Anything. What do you need? I'll get it for you."

She closed her eyes and fought the fear which had her heart beating wildly. "Ric, will you marry me and be the father of my child?"

She watched as shock, disbelief, then rage appeared on his face.

Ric slowly stood with his jaw clenched and asked in a soft, almost deadly, voice, "Who's the bastard that got you pregnant?"

Shaking her head, she replied, "No. No. I'm not pregnant. I want *you* to get me pregnant."

His brown eyes widened, and his jaw grew slack with shock. The expression on his face would have been comical under different circumstances. For the first time in years, she'd truly shocked him.

Anna May held her breath as she waited for his reply. A heartbeat later, he dropped her hand as if it were a live grenade and stepped away from the table, knocking over his chair. "What?" His shock was apparent in the quiet tone of his voice.

"Wait," she said lifting her hand to stop his movement. "This isn't coming out right. Let me start from the beginning."

He reached down to pick up his chair then walked around the table and set it down in front of hers. "All right, start at the beginning," he said as he sat down in the chair with his chest leaning forward and his forearms on his thighs.

He was so close that if she reached out, she could smooth the line between his brows. Another time, another place she would have done exactly that, but fear and nerves made her keep her hands in her lap. Her voice shook as she began to speak.

"Remember two years ago when you came to visit me in the hospital," she continued when he nodded yes. "They removed fibroid tumors from my uterus hoping that they wouldn't return. Two months ago my doctor discovered that tumors were growing again. She suggested I have a child now if I wanted to have one at all. I've thought about it." She paused then added firmly, "I want to have a child."

He ran his hands over his hair. "Have you had a second opinion? Your doctor could be wrong. Have you seen a specialist? Infertile couples are having children all the time. We'll find the best in the business."

Anna May smiled a sad smile. It was so like him to try to fix things for her. "I've had a second and third opinion. They all say the same thing. *Now* is the time to have a child. I can't wait any longer."

"Damn, Anna May," he said as he leaned back in his chair. "There've got to be other options."

"There *aren't* any other options," she replied. "Well, options that I would be able to live with. I'm not involved with anyone, so marriage to someone else is out of the question." She paused then looked down at her tightly clenched hands. "A few of the doctors recommended a sperm bank."

"No! Hell, no." His response was quick and his tone was filled with anger.

She flinched at his tone and met his angry gaze. "I told them I couldn't do that—it seemed so inhuman. Besides, I want my child to know its father not just a list of features I chose from a sperm bank."

He shook his head from side to side. "What kind of quack would even suggest it? If they'd spent any time with you at all, they'd know a sperm bank wasn't an option."

"They're the best doctors in their field," she said quietly.

"And they're telling you that your only hope is to have a child now?"

"Yes."

Silence filled the room. Her heart was beating so fast and hard, she was sure he could hear it.

Slowly he shook his head. "I don't know—"

She interrupted him—afraid, so very afraid, he was about to say no. "I've never asked you for anything before, Ric—but I'm asking you to think about this. Don't give me an answer now," she said when he moved to speak again. "Take a week. Five days to think about it. Please, Ric."

Ric stared at her intently as if memorizing every curve of her face. A deep frown settled on his face, his dark brows drawn together. A tense silence stretched between them. Anna May felt as if a tight band were clamped around her chest, constricting each beat of her heart. He's going to tell me no, she thought. She would lose her only chance to have a child with the man she loved. She wondered if she would also lose her best friend. When she thought she couldn't take the silence any longer, Ric spoke. "All right, I'll think about it."

"Thank you, Ric. This means the world to me."

One corner of his lips lifted in a weak attempt at a smile before he broke eye contact. He bent his head, picked up his fork, and began to eat.

Anna May also picked up her fork and began to move the food around on her plate. Her shoulders relaxed with relief. He hadn't turned her down . . . yet. No answer was better than a flat no.

An uneasy stillness fell between them. Anna May peered at him from beneath her lashes. The frown appeared to deepen as he continued to eat his food. She doubted that he was aware of what he was eating. He was examining every thread of information that she'd given him, searching for a solution that would make them both happy. She'd seen that same expression on his face when he read business reports looking for ways to either save or liquidate a company.

"Ricky?" It had been years since she'd called him that childhood name. His golden brown gaze met hers. "Are we still friends?"

The frown disappeared as he smiled a sad smile at her. "We'll always be friends, Anna May." His voice resounded with conviction, but his eyes were clouded with doubt. Smiling at him in return, she was sure the heaviness that settled in her chest was the pieces of her broken heart.

They sat at the table for another few minutes, each trying to continue the pretense of finishing breakfast. At the sound of Ric's chair sliding across the floor, she stopped playing with her food.

"I've got some reports that I should be reading." He walked to the sink, rinsing off his plate before placing it in the dishwasher. "I'll be in the den if you need anything." He hesitated as if he wanted to say something more—instead he walked out of the room, leaving her alone save for her own thoughts and fears.

The day passed slowly. With the electricity still out, the den was the warmest room in the house. As much as she tried, Anna May couldn't ignore the strain between them. She looked at him from her position on the couch in the den. The magazine that she'd tried to read lay unattended in her lap. Reading was a pitifully weak attempt on her part to curtail her awareness of him. An awareness that would not be denied. On three separate occasions, she found herself watching him read the stack of reports instead of reading the magazine.

He closed his eyes, leaning his head against the soft leather headrest of the easy chair. In the past she would have offered to massage his shoulders to ease the tension in his neck and shoulders. Now she was afraid that he would reject her offer, or if he did accept he would accept out of pity, not friendship. She wasn't going to sit quietly on the couch. They'd been friends for years—surely they could have a civilized conversation.

"Tired?" she asked hoping her voice didn't reveal the longing in her heart.

"Just my eyes. I guess the fire doesn't give off enough light to read," he said rubbing his hand across his face. His eyes weren't the only part of him that was tired, but he couldn't tell her that his whole body ached. Each time that she moved on the couch, his body tensed with anticipation.

Anna May moved with a grace and sensuality of which she was totally unaware. That made him want her all the more. She'd offered him a way to fulfill his desire.

Marriage and a child.

His child.

Of all the men in the world, she wanted him to be the father of her child. It didn't seem fair for her to be in this situation. She was the most caring, giving person he'd ever known. If anyone was more suited to be a mother, it was Anna May. Her home should be filled with children, her children. Children created with a man who loved her. A man who could give her everything she deserved. A man like . . .

He considered the men in her life and systematically dismissed each and every one of them. None of those men would treat her better than he would. None of them would care for her like he could. While he couldn't give her the kind of love she wanted, he could care for her and cherish her better than any man she'd ever dated.

What the hell am I thinking?

Anna May was his best friend. She wanted a child and marriage, the things he'd avoided like the plague.

The faint glow from the fire illuminated her honey brown cheek. Her short, dark brown hair formed a smooth, layered cap around her head. Faint traces of red on her lips were all that was left of the lipstick she'd applied earlier. A thick cream-colored sweater clung to her breasts, and soft brown wool pants, the exact shade of her eyes, hugged her hips. She looked so pretty sitting on the couch. He still couldn't believe that she'd asked *him* to marry her. "Why did she pick me to ask to marry?" He didn't realize that he'd spoken aloud until she answered.

"You have all the qualities that I want for the father of my child. You're intelligent, kind, and a wonderful person."

A wonderful person. She of all people should know

that he wasn't a wonderful person. Hell, sometimes he wasn't even a likable person.

She continued, "You've known me long enough to know that I wouldn't have a child out of wedlock. It goes against everything my parents taught me about God and family. I know that women have children outside of marriage all the time, but I know it's not the right choice for me. We've been friends for a long time. It wouldn't be hard for us to take the next step and become a family."

He felt as if she'd thrown cold water on him.

A family.

He never wanted to be a part of a family again. He wouldn't let himself be hurt that way again.

"We'll never be family, Anna May. Never."

Chapter Three

"Well"—Anna May looked at the ceiling of the den—"I messed that up." The hiss and crackle of the fire broke the silence in the room. Ric had stormed out of the room a few seconds earlier. How could I have been so careless? she wondered. She'd used the "f" word. Family. For as long as she could remember, Ric had had an aversion to anything related to family. Even now, *she* saw more of his aunt and uncle than he did.

After all these years she still couldn't understand why he felt that way. The members of her family were the most important people in her life. She couldn't imagine not being close to her family. Ric on the other hand kept his distance from his relatives. It was as if he wanted to forget his family ever existed.

Anna May folded her legs beneath her and leaned back against the sofa, staring at the cheerful blaze. She'd made a mistake mentioning family. If she wanted him to be the father of her child, she would have to do damage control. First, she would have to make him forget she'd used the word family. Second, she'd have to make him think that getting her pregnant wasn't a bad idea. Neither of the two was going to be easy, but she had to give it a try.

Dinner that evening consisted of soup and sandwiches. Anna May sat on the floor in front of the fireplace, secretly watching Ric eat his dinner. Ric couldn't have chosen a more remote spot without leaving the room, which she was sure he would have done if the power was on and the other rooms weren't ice cold.

If he thinks he can hide over on the other side of the room, he's got another thing coming. She waited until he had taken a sip of his soup before she asked, "Do you think I'm attractive?"

He froze with the spoon poised at his lips. Then he carefully placed the spoon in his bowl. "Yes," he replied cryptically.

"What exactly do you find attractive about me?" she asked before taking a bite of her ham and cheese sandwich. She chewed slowly to hide her smile when she saw him give her a weary, suspicious look.

"Why do you ask?"

"Because I need to know in case you don't want to be the father of my child. I'd like to know what are my best assets to attract a man."

Ric stared at her. Hard. His eyes flashed with annoyance. "This isn't going to work."

"You don't think a man would want me?"

He frowned. "That's not what I said. This exercise of yours isn't going to work."

"What exercise?" she asked blotting her lips with a paper napkin.

"Talking about other men, asking me if I find you attractive. Don't try to manipulate me. I've known you too long for it to work."

"Don't you think I know that? You've just stated the reason why I would never try to manipulate you." She slipped her hand behind her back and crossed her fingers in much the same way as she'd done when she was a child. "We've known each other too long to pull anything over on each other. That's why I'm asking you these questions—because you'll give me a straight answer. Besides you're a man. I need to know what is it about me that you find attractive. I've got to cover all the possibilities in case you decline my offer."

"You make this sound like a business deal," Ric muttered.

"It is a business deal of sorts. I get the child I want and you get . . ." Her voice trailed off as she looked away from his gaze.

"Yes, what do I get out of this?"

Slowly she turned to him. "Whatever you want, Ric. I'd be forever in your debt."

"Don't be so quick to put yourself in debt without first knowing the total cost. It might be more than you can afford," he said in a soft, almost distracted voice.

"You'd never ask for more than I could give," Anna May said quietly.

Ric's frown deepened.

Seeing his frown, Anna May pasted a smile on her face. "We've gotten totally off the subject, and you still haven't answered my question. What do you find attractive about me?"

He took another sip of his soup and carefully studied her. "You have a cute face."

"Cute?" she asked in disbelief.

"Yeah. Cute."

Anna May shook her head. "No, Ric. Babies are cute. Puppies are cute. Grown women aren't cute."

"Look, you asked me a question and I've given you my answer," he replied with a laugh.

"I don't want to be cute," she said in frustration. "I want to be attractive, sexy, dangerous. Cute is so . . . so tame."

Ric shook his head in confusion. "There's nothing wrong with cute. I like cute."

"Uh-huh. Then why do you date women who look like they should be on the cover of *Essence* magazine?"

"I am not going to apologize for dating beautiful women."

"See there," Anna May pointed her finger at him.

He held up his hands in confusion. "What?"

"You didn't call them cute."

"Anna May, give me a break," he said folding his arms across his chest.

"I've got one more question. Do you know any single men?"

"Yes. Why?"

"If you won't marry me and give me a child, maybe you know someone who will."

Ric couldn't sleep. Anna May had fallen asleep within minutes after lying down. He, on the other hand, stared at the shadows on the ceiling, wide awake. How could he fall asleep with her lying at his side? Her lush body so close to his. The sweet smell of her jasmine perfume stirring his senses and his manhood.

He wanted so badly to skirt his hands around her neat little waist, then glide them over her firm hips and stomach. Her stomach which would grow large with child, his child, if she had her way.

He'd never considered having a child. Building his company had required most of his time. Dating was a luxury he couldn't afford then. Now that it was successful, he was very selective when dating. He'd seen more than one successful businessman trapped by a money-hungry woman. If he hadn't known Anna May for so long, he would have thought she was trying to get his money. She'd turned down all of his offers to help her financially. He could have made her a rich woman many times over, but she wasn't interested.

He tensed as she moved on the other side of the sofa bed then relaxed when she stayed on her side. He was already hugging the edge of the sofa. If he moved any more, he'd be on the floor. He wished there was a way to give her the child that she wanted without getting involved with her. Ric smiled in the darkness. Immaculate conception was a one-time deal as far as he knew, and unless things had changed in the last few weeks, Anna May was definitely a virgin. She was also stubborn and determined. He didn't doubt she'd do everything she could to marry and have a child. She'd offered to be forever in his debt. Didn't she realize giving her a child would clear the debt he owed her? A life for a life. She'd saved his life and he could give her a child, a life in return.

As he stared into the darkness, he wondered if he could afford the price.

* * *

Three days later . . .

Anna May placed the last tray of fruit on her oak dining room table and surveyed the spread. Fresh fruit, lean meats, and steamed vegetables were arranged on the table. It was her turn to host the monthly meeting of the Ladies' Club.

She and Janet Hill had formed the group out of self-defense. They were the only women in their company's public relations department. They'd supported each other when their male co-workers were promoted over them, used each other as a sounding board for ideas, and helped each other plan their careers. Raina Deux and Marianne Jones became members of the club two years later when they came to work for the company.

In the four years since they began meeting, they'd seen Marianne and Janet leave the company to join other firms. They'd planned Marianne's wedding and later her baby shower, been at Anna May's side at her surgery two years ago, and supported Marianne during a very nasty divorce.

Anna May adjusted a tray of vegetables on the table. I hope that they'll support me when I tell them about my plan with Ric, she thought. Ric. She hadn't expected him to distance himself from her. She'd invited him out for dinner like she would have done any other time, but he'd declined. He said it was because he was working late, but she could tell from his tone that he wasn't being truthful. That had hurt.

At the sound of the doorbell, she smoothed the fabric of her gray wool pants over her hips and straightened her shoulders. She paused before the mirror in the foyer, checking her appearance, then asked, "Who is it?"

"Janet."

Anna May opened the door. Janet Hill stood on the porch, holding a bunch of flowers. When people saw Janet for the first time, they thought she was a teenager until they noticed her eyes. She had the kind of eyes that had seen too much.

"Hey, girl." Janet stepped inside, giving Anna May the flowers. "These are for you."

"Thanks. They're gorgeous." She had learned over the years to accept Janet's small gifts when she came to her home. Janet never came to anyone's home empty handed.

"Do you need any help with the food?" Janet asked as she took off her coat.

Anna May laid the flowers on the table in the foyer. "No. I've got everything taken care of. Do you want anything to drink while we wait for the others to get here?"

"The regular. Water with lemon." Janet looked around the room. "You've changed things around again," she said.

"Yeah." Anna May looked around her living room. "The look in this room was getting old. It needed something fresh. What do you think?"

Janet tilted her head to the side and surveyed the room. "It's okay but seems a little too tame for you."

"That's what I told Ric when he helped me move the furniture."

"Ah, that explains it," Janet said.

"Explains what?"

"You wouldn't have chosen this look on your own. It's not bright, and there's not enough color."

"I like this," Anna May said defensively.

Janet put her hands into the pockets of her baggy jeans and shrugged her shoulders. "Whatever you say."

The doorbell rang. Anna May went to the door.

"Hey"—Marianne hugged her then rushed through the door—"I'm so sorry we're late."

"It wasn't your fault, Marianne," Raina said quietly as she walked inside. "The Department of Transportation closed the exit that we normally use, and the side streets were crowded."

"That's okay," Anna May said. "You're here now."

"No, it's not okay," Marianne said. "I made a bet with Janet that I'd get here on time. For once, I left early so I could arrive at our meeting on time. Now I have to pay Janet twenty dollars."

"I take Visa, MasterCard, American Express—and yes, of course, cash," Janet said from her position in the recliner.

Marianne sighed then reached inside her purse.

"I don't know why you bet with Janet. You always lose," Anna May said.

"One of these days I'm going to win," Marianne replied.

"We'll all be old and retired when that happens," Janet said.

Shaking her head, Anna May joined her friends.

"You've been moving stuff around again," Raina said. "I like it. It's very cool, very sophisticated."

"Thank you." Anna May smiled.

"It's pretty, but it just doesn't seem like you," Marianne interjected.

Anna May glared at Janet.

"I didn't say anything to her," Janet said holding up her hands in surrender.

Marianne looked back and forth between them in confusion. "What?" she asked.

"Ric helped me with this room," Anna May replied.

"This looks like his style," Raina said as she looked around the room. "Controlled and orderly."

"It looks just fine," Anna May insisted, dipping a carrot stick into the low-fat dressing.

"I'll bet you twenty dollars she'll change this room in two weeks," Janet said.

"That's not a bet," Marianne replied. "That's a sure thing."

"Maybe we should bet on the color she'll use in this room." Janet sipped her water with lemon.

"No. I think we—"

"If you two don't mind," Anna May said interrupting Marianne, "I'd like to talk to you about something important."

"What is it?" Raina asked.

Anna May looked at her friends, trying to force the words from her lips. It was hard, almost as hard as it had been to tell Ric. She knew they would share her hurt, her anger, and when she needed it, they would share their strength and love. "I went to the doctor a few weeks ago." She closed her eyes in an effort to stem the tears. Her effort was in vain. "The tumors are back."

In seconds they were at her side.

"Oh, no." Marianne reached out and held her hand.

"What did the doctor say?" Janet demanded while Raina quietly waited for her answer.

"I actually saw three different doctors, and they all say the same thing. If I'm going to have a child, I need to get pregnant now."

"What are you going to do, Anna May?" Raina asked quietly and pressed a napkin in her hand.

She wiped her cheeks and eyes with the napkin. "I've thought and prayed about this, and I hope you'll support my decision."

"What's your decision?" Janet asked.

Anna May looked at her friends then said, "I've decided to get married and have a child."

"But you're not dating anybody," Marianne said in confusion.

Raina frowned.

Janet pinned her with a piercing glare. "Unless you know something that we don't," she said gesturing to Raina and Marianne. "You don't just decide to get married and have a child like you decide to have ketchup on a hamburger."

"I didn't just up and decide to get married. I made a list of all the things I wanted in a husband and father, then I made a list of all the men I thought would meet those criteria. That's when I came to my decision."

"Wait a minute," Janet said. "You made a list like you would if you were going grocery shopping, then picked a man?"

"You didn't have to say it like that, but . . . yes. That's what I did," Anna May replied.

"Who did you decide on?" Raina asked.

"I've asked Ric to marry me." Anna May folded her hands in her lap and waited for the explosion. She didn't have long to wait.

"What?" Marianne gasped.

"Oh," Raina mused.

"The Ice Man," Janet said as she nodded her head.

"This is not right, Anna May," Marianne said coming to her feet. "This isn't the way to start a marriage.

It's not the way to bring a child into the world. Marriage is hard enough, even when two people love each other.''

"I love Ric."

"But does he love you?" Marianne asked. "It's hell being married to a man who doesn't love you, Anna May. I know what it's like. Don't make the same mistake I made."

"I know Ric doesn't love me," she said. "I don't have the time to wait on love. It's now or never as far as time to have a child."

"Have you talked with your family?" Raina asked.

"No, not yet. I'm waiting to hear Ric's decision."

"When will you hear from him?" Janet asked.

"Tomorrow."

"I don't know about this," Marianne muttered.

"Ya'll are my closest friends, and I need your support right now." Anna May looked at her friends.

"We'll support you," Janet said. "Whatever you decide to do, we'll be there for you. Right?" She looked at Raina and Marianne.

"Right," Raina added with a soft smile.

Marianne gave her a concerned frown before reluctantly replying, "Right."

Anna May felt as if a weight had been lifted off her shoulders. She hadn't realized how much the support of her friends meant to her until that moment. Now all she had to do was wait on Ric's decision.

"Do you think Ric will marry you?" Raina asked.

"I don't know, Raina. I don't know."

"Well, it seems to me that you need to start planning this wedding," Janet said from across the room.

"I've already looked into it," Anna May said. "But the courthouse would be much faster."

"You don't really think your family is going to let

their only girl slide by with a courthouse wedding, do you?" Marianne said.

"No. I want a church wedding, but I've got to start trying to have a child as soon as possible."

"She has a point, Marianne," Raina said softly. "If I were a virgin at thirty-three years old, I'd want to have sex real soon, too."

Anna May stared at Raina in surprise. Laughter bubbled up inside her. She put her hand over her lips to hold back the laughter, but she lost the battle at the sound of Janet's unladylike guffaw.

"I'm a virgin and I'm proud of it," Anna May said when she finally stopped laughing.

"You aren't going to be a virgin for long if you want to have a baby," Janet said.

No, Anna May thought to herself. I won't be a virgin for long. I hope.

Janet joined Raina and Marianne at Marianne's house a few hours later. Marianne's three-year-old daughter, Noriah, wrapped her arms around Janet's knees as soon as Janet entered the room.

"Hi," Noriah said. "Have you come to play with me?"

"Uh . . ." Janet looked down at the little girl, who was now using her legs for balance as she leaned back to look at her.

"Honey, she'll play with you in a few minutes." Marianne unlatched her daughter from Janet's legs. "Mama, Janet, and Raina need to talk."

"What are you talking about?" Noriah asked.

Marianne tickled Noriah's belly. "We're going to talk about you."

"You are?"

"No," she said. "Why don't I put on a dinosaur tape?

"Raina's in the living room, Janet. It won't take me long to get Noriah settled."

Janet walked into the living room and joined Raina on the sofa. "Why do I let a three-year-old scare me?"

"I'm convinced Noriah is really twenty years old," Raina said.

Marianne joined them. "That tape should hold her for about forty-five minutes," she said as she sat in a chair. "Janet, we've got to stop Anna May from going through with this crazy plan of hers."

"Whoa, whoa," Janet said frowning. "You said you'd give her your support a few hours ago."

"I know, but I can't just sit back and let her make a mess of her life."

Janet turned to Raina. "Do you feel the same way?"

"No. Whatever Anna May decides to do, I'll support her. She's been in love with Ric for years. Maybe this will work for them," Raina said.

"I can't believe the two of you," Marianne snapped. "Our friend is about to make the worst mistake of her life, and you two are going to go along with it."

"We can't stop Anna May from doing what she thinks is best," Janet said. "Like we couldn't stop you from getting married to a known womanizer."

"That's exactly why we've got to stop her," Marianne insisted.

"That's exactly why we're going to let her make her own decision," Raina said. "Anna May has to do what's right for her, like we have to do what's right for us. If you push her, she'll push back hard. Do you really want to lose her friendship over this?"

Marianne shook her head. "I don't want to lose her friendship, but I can't help but be concerned."

"We are all concerned," Janet added. "I'm afraid Ric won't marry her. I'm afraid Ric *will* marry her and break her heart."

"All we can do," Raina said gently, "is be her friend right now and wait and see what happens."

The three women silently contemplated the weeks ahead. For different reasons, they were all afraid for Anna May.

"Good morning, Mr. Justice."

"Morning, Mrs. Jones." Ric walked past his secretary's desk and into his plush eighteenth-floor office. In the five years since he'd hired her, he'd never called her by her first name. He'd always called her Mrs. Jones, and she always referred to him as Mr. Justice. They'd never developed the informal business relationship like some of his junior officers had with their secretaries, and he preferred to keep it that way.

Over the years he'd fired more than one secretary for being too free with information on him, both personal and business. Mrs. Jones had lasted the longest, but he was still very careful to not invite a closer working relationship.

Thick gray carpet muffled the sound of his footsteps. His office consisted of three rooms: a conference room, a full bath, and the room where he did most of his work. Ric felt the view from his office windows was wasted on him. He never had time to look out the windows. With the exception of his laptop computer, printer, and telephone, most of the furnishings in his office were wasted on him. A plain metal desk instead of the solid mahogany desk would have suited him. He'd learned to tolerate, if not ignore, the sometimes frivolous trappings of success.

Placing his computer in the docking station, he skimmed the fax which lay on his desk and smiled in satisfaction. His attention was diverted when a series of beeps from his computer signaled reception of his electronic mail messages. He quickly scanned the messages until he read the message he'd sent to himself. It read: *Give Anna May an answer tonight.*

What was he going to say to her? Yes, I'll marry you and be the father of your child. Man, woman, and child.

A family.

He had enough family as it was with his aunt, uncle, and half brother. He'd learned early in life that family will betray you. His father had left him and his mother to fight in Vietnam and was killed. His mother sent him to live with his grandmother when she remarried and had never looked back. He wouldn't have known she'd died if he hadn't seen her obituary in the newspaper. His grandmother had taken the money his mother had given her to raise him and spent it on her weekly supply of wine.

When he moved in with his aunt and uncle, he had learned his lesson about family and kept himself distant from them. He didn't want any more family.

But how could he say no to the woman who was his one and only true friend? A woman who'd given him hope and friendship when others had given up on him. The one person who believed in him, sometimes when he hadn't believed in himself. The woman who'd hounded the firemen fighting a fire at his college dorm until one of them carried him from the burning building. He'd been unconscious when they'd brought him out, and if it hadn't been for her, he could have been one of the students who'd died in the fire.

With a single keystroke, he deleted the message. He had to come to a decision soon. Over the last four days, he'd grown less sure that he could tell her no.

"Mr. Morgan is here, Mr. Justice." His secretary's voice interrupted his thoughts.

"Send him in," Ric answered.

Warren Morgan, his senior business manager, entered the room. Morgan carried himself with the quiet confidence of a much older man. Ric had often wondered if Morgan's wealthy upbringing was the reason for his confidence. Morgan didn't need his salary. His father had given him enough money to permanently retire at the age of twenty-five. "Good morning, Mr. Justice."

"Morgan," Ric replied as he stepped around his desk to join him at the small conference table where Morgan began removing manila files from his briefcase.

"You were right about Jamison," Morgan said. "He's been embezzling from his company for years and writing off the losses. I think we should hold off on our offer to buy his company until I can find out the extent of the damage."

"Fine. Jamison's company is good, but there are other good companies. What's next?"

Morgan opened another file. "Renoylds and Associates. Rusty Renoylds isn't a happy man. He likes being in charge. Now that he's no longer the largest stockholder, he could turn ugly."

"Mr. Renoylds knew the risks when he released his stock options," Ric replied.

"True, but he's making noises of conspiracy to anyone who'll listen to him."

"We'll work around him. When Renoylds and Associates is profitable again, I'm sure he'll quiet down."

"Next is Wilson and Wilson. It's a regional consulting firm. The founder recently stepped down, and his son is now running the business. Good thing because the old man almost went bankrupt last year. The son has made some very savvy moves to keep the company afloat, but the company's so far in debt, he won't be able to get out of it without backing."

"What's the son's name?" Ric asked.

Morgan shuffled a few sheets of paper then said, "His name is Adam Wilson. Actually, he bought out the father nine months ago. He's young, only twenty-seven years old, but he'd be good to keep if we bought him out."

Ric leaned back in his chair. He hadn't heard that name in a long time. "A twenty-seven-year-old bought out his father? How?"

"Instead of going to work for his father, Adam Wilson went to work for a small engineering firm. Apparently he made a deal with the owners to have a part of his salary in shares of the company. Wilson and the owner implemented improvements, and the company almost doubled its profits the next year. By then Wilson had a forty percent ownership in the company. That same year he and his partner held out against a hostile takeover. For someone his age, he has had to make some hard decisions, and it's made him a tough businessman."

"Sounds good. Keep me informed on this deal."

"Right," Morgan said closing the folder. "The company's history and a little of the owner's background is in this file. If we can buy this company, I think it will be profitable within months."

Later when Morgan left his office, Ric sat at his

desk and opened the Wilson file. He skimmed over the business report and stopped when he came to an old newspaper clipping. It was dated last year. Ric picked up the clipping and stared at the threesome. An older man and woman sat side by side next to a table full of gifts. A younger man stood behind them. It was the first time he'd seen his mother and half brother in nearly twenty-seven years.

Chapter Four

Anna May watched as Noriah gripped the long-handled wooden spoon with both hands and stirred the chocolate cake mixture with all her might. Dark brown stains spotted her old white cotton shirt, which she'd used as a makeshift apron for the three-year-old. Matching brown stains dotted Anna May's kitchen counter.

"Boy, you're doing a great job, Noriah. I don't see any lumps, do you?" Anna May smiled as Noriah leaned over the bowl and thoroughly studied the cake mix.

"I don't see any lumps," she declared while still looking into the bowl.

"Come on, let's put this in the pan." With Noriah's help, two pans of cakes were filled and put into the oven.

"Are we gonna cook something else?"

"In a little while, sweetie," she said running the back of her hand over Noriah's upturned face. Anna

May felt a lump in her throat as she looked at her. Her baby-fine hair was parted down the middle, forming two fluffy Afro puffs. Dark brown eyes, full of curiosity, were looking to her with joy, trust, and wonder. Wonder—which children seemed to have an unending supply of.

Anna May longed to have a child of her own to love and nurture all the time, not for small blocks of time when she was baby-sitting like tonight. She wanted to feel her child growing inside her. She wanted to watch it grow and discover the world. She wanted all of that. But she didn't know if it would ever come to pass.

It was five days ago when she'd asked Ric to father her child, and he'd yet to contact her.

A small sticky hand patted her leg. "What are we going to do now?"

"We are going to wash our hands, then we're going to play one of your video games." She was interrupted by the sound of the doorbell. Noriah climbed down from the chair she had been standing on and ran to the door. "I'll get it. I'll get it."

"Noriah," Anna May said firmly following her out of the kitchen. "Don't touch the door." She had a dead bolt on the front door which could be unlocked only with a key. Noriah had a habit of trying to open the front door at home, and Marianne was trying to teach her not to open doors without permission.

When she'd reached the front door, Noriah was hopping from one leg to the other waiting for her arrival. Anna May made a note to reward her for her behavior, then looked through the peephole.

Ric stood on the other side of the door. Anticipation and dread filled her at the sight of him. She put her hand on the knob, then remembered the curious child watching every move she made. "Who is it?" she asked for Noriah's benefit.

"Ric."

The cold air chilled her when she opened the door, but she was instantly warmed when Ric walked inside. His caramel wool coat emphasized his broad shoulders and lean hips. Anna May felt a tingle of excitement in her stomach, and her heart beat faster as his warm brown eyes met hers. An aura of strength surrounded him from the firm, chiseled angles of his cheeks to the chest-out, shoulders-back way he stood in the room. He was a very attractive man and she wanted him.

"Who's that man, Anna May?" Noriah's childlike voice broke the sensual web which had formed around them.

With a mental shake, she said, "This is Mr. Justice, honey. He's my friend."

Noriah looked from Ric to Anna May, then stepped behind Anna May to hide her face. She took a quick peek at him and hid her face again.

Anna May smiled at Ric. "She's feeling a little shy tonight." She ran her hand over Noriah's hair. "Don't be shy. Mr. Justice is really nice." Her words coaxed the little girl from her hiding place, and Noriah stared at Ric with solemn dark brown eyes.

Ric kneeled in front of her and smiled. "Hello. What's your name?"

Noriah looked at Anna May, waiting for permission to speak to him.

"Go ahead. Tell him your name."

"Noriah Jeaan Jones," she replied softly.

"Nice to meet you, Noriah Jeaan Jones," he said holding out his hand. She stepped forward, placing her tiny hand in his, and swung her arm above her head then pumped twice.

"Are you Anna May's boyfriend?" she asked.

Out of the mouths of babes, Anna May thought. She purposely focused on Noriah so she wouldn't see Ric's expression. "Mr. Justice is a man, and he's my friend—so I guess he is my boyfriend."

Noriah gave her a puzzled look. "But if he's a man, wouldn't he be a manfriend?"

"There's no such word as manfriend," Anna May replied. "You could say friend, and that would cover everybody whether they are a man, woman, boy or girl."

"Oh," she said with a frown.

Ric rose from his kneeling position, his expression apologetic. "I didn't realize you had company. I should have called first."

"That's okay," she said then glanced at her watch. "Marianne should be here in about an hour. If you want to wait, you can."

"We made cake," Noriah interjected as if to convince him to stay.

Ric smiled at her. "In that case, I'll stay." Noriah gave him a coquettish grin.

Anna May smiled at him. "We were about to play video games. I've got to avenge myself. Noriah beat the stuffing out of me the last game."

"Can he play? Can he play? I wanna play with him," Noriah said.

"Why don't we show him how to play first, then he'll play a game with you," Anna May said. As the three of them walked to the den, Noriah walked between them, holding their hands. It was a scene Anna May had witnessed many times before, a child holding her parents' hands. A hunger and longing filled her, and she felt her throat tighten. This was what she wanted. A husband and a child.

Ric watched as Anna May, along with Noriah's "help," attached the game piece to the television. She lovingly guided small hands to the correct place on the game piece and carefully answered questions as if they were talking friend to friend rather than adult to child. She was great with the little girl, he thought. He had always pictured her with a husband and children, yet he'd never asked her why she hadn't married. Maybe he should have.

"Come watch us play, Ric," Anna May said then smiled at him. He sat on the floor behind the two. He knew he had only one choice to make.

"Bye, Anna May. Bye." Noriah waved her free hand with her mother, Marianne, holding the other.

"Thanks again for watching Noriah," Marianne said as she stood in the foyer, looking toward the den where Ric was reconnecting the cables to her television. "I hope she didn't interrupt anything. If I'd have known you were having company, I would have found another sitter."

"It's okay, Marianne. She was no problem at all."

Marianne looked at her, her brow wrinkled and her expression worried. "Have you guys made a decision yet?"

"No," Anna May replied. "Not yet."

Marianne bit her lower lip, a sure sign that something was bothering her. "Call me if you need anything. Anything at all, okay?"

"I will."

Looking at her daughter she said, "Put your gloves on, snooky. It's cold outside."

Anna May stood in the doorway and watched as the two got into their car. She waved when Marianne blew her horn, then closed the door.

Ric was packing away the game when she walked into the den. "Well, they're gone."

Ric nodded his head. "I can tell. It's a lot quieter."

She laughed then said, "I never realize how quiet it is until she leaves."

"Does she always ask that many questions? Maybe the police should use children to interrogate people."

"She always asks questions. She's a smart little girl and very curious about the things around her. I love having her over."

Ric nodded slowly, his eyes grew dark and serious. "I can tell."

Anna May felt her heart beat a little faster. Now that they were alone, there was no reason for them to put off their talk. "Do you want anything to drink before we get started?" she asked.

"No, I'm fine."

"Well," she said walking to the leather recliner. "Have you made a decision?" She was surprised to hear her voice sounding smooth and calm when she was shaking inside.

"I think we need to talk first," he replied walking to the matching chair beside hers. "I've got a few questions."

"What do you want to know?" she asked rubbing her palms along the top of her blue jean-clad thighs.

"Do you know if you can get pregnant?"

"Yes, I've had some tests run. My doctor feels there's no reason why I couldn't have a child."

Ric nodded as if to digest the information. "How do you plan to get pregnant? With a test tube or the old-fashioned way?"

Anna May felt heat rush to her face. "The old-fashioned way."

"What happens if you don't get pregnant right away?"

"Are you asking how long we should try before we give up?"

He frowned then said, "Yes."

"A year."

His frown deepened. "What happens once you have the child?"

"What do you mean?"

"I mean, am I supposed to disappear from the child's life and yours?"

"Oh, no," she said shaking her head. "I want you to be an active part of the baby's life. I would never ask you to disappear. If you want, we can have a prenuptial agreement with that in it. I'd like to have one anyway because I want it spelled out that you keep everything you have now as far as money is concerned."

"We'll come back to that. What about joint custody?"

"That can go into the prenup."

"You haven't asked me any questions. I think there are some things you should know about me."

She shrugged her shoulders. "Like what? I know the most important things."

"Have I practiced safe sex? The answer is yes, always. Am I in good health? Yes. I had a complete physical two months ago, including a sperm count and an AIDS test. I can give a baby."

Anna May felt heat rush to her face as embarrassment enveloped her. Even as she shifted in her chair, her love for him grew a little more. Ric wanted her to know she was safe with him. "I never doubted that you could give me a child. Isn't it silly considering my situation and AIDS." She paused to gather her composure. "AIDS never crossed my mind."

"It should have. Knowledge could mean the difference between life and death."

"I know, and you don't have to worry about me. I'm still a virgin."

"Okay. Then the only other question is when do you want to get married?"

Anna May gasped. "Do you mean it?"

"I mean it," he said coming to his feet.

She rushed out of her chair and hugged him. "Oh, Ricky," she said as the tears formed in her eyes. "You won't regret this, I promise."

He was beginning to regret his decision to marry her, and the night wasn't over yet. "Anna May, I don't remember the last time I was in church. I don't see why we can't go to the justice of the peace."

"This may not be the most romantic wedding in the world, but I'm getting married in front of God and everybody," she said crossing her arms across her chest. She had that stubborn-as-a-mule look on her face. He'd come across that expression once or twice, and he knew she wasn't going to budge on this issue.

"It will take longer if we have a church wedding," he replied. "If we go the justice of the peace, we can be married within a week. I thought time was of the essence."

"It is, but my dad will marry us if I ask him, and

we can use my church's chapel. It's practically empty on Saturdays. Winter isn't a popular time for weddings."

"You've already made plans with the church?"

"I didn't make plans," she said. "All I did was ask if the chapel was available on Saturdays. The secretary showed me the calendar."

"Fine," he said realizing he'd lost that point. "What are you going to tell your family about this marriage?"

"I'm going to tell them the truth. It'll be much easier in the long run if they know up front this marriage is temporary."

"They won't like this."

"I know, but they love me and sooner and later they will come around."

Ric wasn't so sure. He'd seen firsthand what families did to each other. He made a mental note to be present when her family arrived.

"When are you going to tell them about us?"

"I could call my parents right now."

"Call them," he said. He waited in silence as she made the call to her parents' home in California, ready to give her his support when her family disappointed her.

"Hi, Mom," she said a few seconds later. "Is Daddy there? Good, put him on the phone with you. Hi, Daddy. I'm fine. Listen"—she paused and looked at him from across the room—"I've got some news for you."

He noticed she didn't say *good* news.

"No, Mom. I'm not moving to California. I'm getting married to Ric Justice. What? Wait. Don't talk at the same time. No, we haven't been dating long. Yes, this is rather soon but— Sure, Daddy, I want you to talk to him face-to-face. Well, he's standing right here. I know marriage is a big step and . . . I'm sure this is what I want. No, we haven't set a date yet, but it will be soon. How soon? Two to three weeks. I . . . but . . . We don't want to wait. No, he's not pushing me. I'm the one who wants to get married so soon because I want to have a child right away. Daddy!''

He'd heard enough. Ric walked to her side and motioned for the phone.

"Ric wants to talk to you," she said and gave him the phone.

"Hello, Mr. and Mrs. Robinson."

"Young man," Reverend Steven Robinson began, his voice booming, "what is going on?"

"Sir, Anna May and I have decided to get married, and we want to do it soon. We'd like for you to be present at the ceremony."

"Why the rush?" her mother interjected. "There's no reason to rush, is there?"

"She's not pregnant, is she?" her father asked in a shocked tone.

"No," Ric replied. At least not yet, he thought to himself.

"Then there's no reason why you can't wait a few months," her father said.

"We don't want to wait," he said with a hint of steel in his voice. "Anna May and I will be married in a few weeks. She wants you to perform the ceremony. Will you do it?"

Ric looked into Anna May's anxious face as he waited for her father's answer. Silence stretched on the telephone line. He tensed as if to prepare himself for a physical blow. He'd tried to warn her, and now she was going to be hurt by her family. The least he could do was soften the blow when her father refused. The silence ended when her father spoke.

"Thank you, sir," Ric replied surprised at the answer. "It is very important to Anna May. Hold on, she wants to talk to you."

She took the phone and Ric wandered to the other side of the room. He was engaged, he thought in wonder. In a few weeks he would be married. Have a wife. Anna May Justice. She looked in his direction as if he'd said her name aloud. Her brown eyes were alive with happiness. She should be happy, he thought. She was getting what she'd asked for. Him and later his child.

Ric put his hands in his pants pockets. He never really had a choice in the matter. She was his best friend, and he cared for her more than anyone else in the world.

"Thank goodness that's over," she said sitting in the recliner with her elbows on her knees, supporting her head with her hands.

"Why didn't you tell them about the tumors?" he asked. "It might have made it easier for you."

"I'll tell them tomorrow. I don't think they could take hearing about it right now."

"Are you free for lunch tomorrow?"

"I think so."

"Good. We'll pick out rings and make an appointment to get the marriage certificate and blood tests."

An engagement ring. As much as she wanted her marriage to be real in every sense of the word, she didn't want to take advantage of his generosity. "A plain gold band will be fine with me. Don't spend a lot of money on me."

"That won't do. Occasionally I have to meet clients in a social setting along with their wives and I don't want you to feel uncomfortable when people ask to see the ring and you don't have one."

"Oh, I didn't think of that," she said, her brow furled in a frown. "My family might think it was strange, too. Do you want to call your aunt and uncle now?"

"No."

"I suppose we could go see them tomorrow and give them the news," she said.

"No, that's all right. I'll tell them."

"You don't want me to be with you when you tell them?"

"Don't make a big deal out of this. My aunt and uncle probably could care less if I got married."

On the other side of the country, Steven and Carolyn Robinson tried to come to grips with the news their only daughter had given them.

"Something's wrong," Carolyn said.

"Of course, something's wrong. Our daughter's getting married in haste," Steven replied.

"No, there's more to this than what she's telling us."

"Ric," he said still dazed from the telephone call, "said she wasn't pregnant. Why would they lie about it? We can count to nine like anybody else."

"I've got a feeling about this, Steven. Anna May's impulsive, but this doesn't sound like her. I'm going to call James and Steven Jr. Maybe they'll know what's going on."

"We would have heard about it if either of our sons knew what was going on."

"I'm going to call them anyway," Carolyn said as she picked up the telephone.

Carla Fredd

Steven listened with half an ear as his wife spoke with their youngest son, James. He could tell from her comments that James didn't know any more than they did about Anna May's upcoming marriage. The same was true with Steven Jr.

"They don't know what's happening, either. James said she didn't say anything to him when he flew down last week," Carolyn said.

"We'll know soon enough," he replied. "I'm going to fix some coffee. Do you want a cup?"

"Yes," she said with a sigh.

He walked into the kitchen and began to prepare the coffee. As the stream of brown liquid poured into the pot, he stared at the telephone.

A few minutes later with a cup in each hand, he entered the den where his wife was waiting. "Pack a bag, Carolyn. We're going to Atlanta tomorrow."

"Ric," Anna May said in a fierce whisper. "I told you I didn't want an expensive ring." She glanced toward the open door where the jeweler went to bring another collection of stones. Ric told the man the stones they'd seen weren't exactly what they were looking for, larger stones were what they had in mind.

"It won't be an expensive ring," he replied.

"It won't be expensive for who? Ted Turner?" she whispered.

"He's coming back."

The jeweler entered the private room holding yet another black case. "I think this set of stones is what you're looking for," he said. He removed several envelopes from the case, then opened them.

She gasped. The stones were more beautiful than

any she'd seen so far. She picked up a large pear-shaped diamond.

"That's an excellent stone," the man said. "Four and a half carats—very, very fine."

"We'll take it," Ric said.

"Ric!"

Twenty minutes later they left the store with a promise from the jeweler that her ring would be sized, set, and ready for delivery that evening.

The next stop was Emory Hospital for their blood test. He'd managed to convince his doctor to put a rush on their test results, and they would have them within the hour. That is, if Anna May held up that long.

"Do we have to get this done today? Tomorrow is good for me," Anna May said for the third time as they waited in the lobby.

He took her cold hands in his. "It's okay. You don't have to be afraid."

She lifted her chin and said without hesitation, "I'm not afraid."

Her show of bravado was undermined as her hands began to tremble. She'd had that same look on her face in college when he'd taken her to the emergency room. She hadn't cried when the glass she was washing shattered in her hand, but she cried like a baby when the doctor gave her a shot to ease her pain. Anna May was terrified of needles.

"Anna May Robinson." A lab-coat-clad technician called her name. Her hand clamped around his like a vise, and her eyes widened with fear.

"I'll come with you," he said softly. "I won't let them hurt you."

Together they walked toward the technician. The young man looked from Anna May's terrified expression to Ric's determined face. He smiled. "Ms. Robinson, why don't you have a seat over there while I get your friend a chair."

"O . . . okay," she replied, her voice trembling.

Ric sat down next to her and held her hand. "So tell me about this press release you've got to finish." He had to keep her talking. Next to her family and friends, her job as a public relations consultant was her favorite topic of conversation.

"I . . . I can't tell you about this one."

"Oh? The last time you said that the price of your company's stock went up ten percent. Should I buy more shares?" She flinched as the needle pierced her skin. Ric gave the technician a killing glare. The young man swallowed nervously.

"So what are your parents up to? Have you talked to your brothers lately?" Talking about her job wasn't distracting her, but talking about her family would keep her mind off what was happening. He normally avoided talking about her family but he'd do just about anything to take away her fears.

"I haven't talked to either of them," she said softly, her frightened gaze never leaving his. He kept her talking until the young man was finished. Ric walked with her to the lobby, making sure she was all right before rejoining the technician who was waiting to take his blood.

Her color had improved by the time he returned to the lobby, and she even smiled at him.

"Thanks for staying with me," she said.

He smiled at her in return. "Hey, what are friends for?"

She took his hand and held it until their results were ready an hour later.

* * *

"Can we eat now?" she asked when they'd reached his dark green Jaguar convertible. Their marriage license along with their test results were now in her possession.

Ric was like a man on a mission this afternoon. He was treating their wedding with the same organizational skill he used in his normal business activities. It was as if he had a mental checklist. Engagement ring. Check. Blood test. Check. Marriage license. Check. Anna May hadn't decided if she was happy with his actions or not.

"Sure. What do you have in mind for lunch?" he asked.

"I want a naked dog with a big F.O.," she said with a smile.

The Varsity was the only place in Atlanta where it was normal for naked dogs to be ordered. Anna May picked up their order for two plain hot dogs and a frosted orange shake and searched for Ric, who'd found an empty table for them to sit at.

She unwrapped the hot dog, took a bite, and closed her eyes in delight. "They serve the best hot dogs."

"I hope you feel this way later on tonight when the grease has had a chance to settle," Ric replied.

"If you don't want that hot dog, I'll eat it."

"I didn't say I wasn't going to eat," he said while unwrapping his hot dog.

"You're just trying to make me feel guilty for eating this fat- and calorie-filled lunch—well, it ain't gonna happen," she said after sipping her frosted orange. "Besides, I've been eating healthy for the last few months, and I can afford this one little indulgence." She paused as a young couple sat at the table beside them. The woman was obviously in the later stages of pregnancy. Anna May felt a twinge of envy as the woman placed her husband's hand over her stomach. Feeling as if she were intruding on a private moment, she looked away.

"When are you planning to move your things?" Ric asked.

"What things?" she asked.

"Your clothes, some furniture. I'm assuming you want to move to my house since it's the biggest. Am I wrong?"

"Oh, no. You're not wrong." Sometimes when she'd indulged herself in fantasy, she'd dreamed of living in his home and becoming his wife. Now for a brief time her dream would come true. She would have the right to lie in the huge four-poster mahogany bed beside him. To make a child together. She shivered at the thought as sparks of desire raced throughout her body. "I'll start packing some of my things this weekend and ask Janet if she wants to live in my house for a year. She's been complaining about her apartment complex lately."

"Let me know if you need any help, and I'll make a point to come over," he said as he looked at his watch. "We'd better go. I've got a two o'clock meeting."

He dropped her off in front of her office building in the heart of town. "I'll see you tonight," he said when he brought the car to a halt.

"You don't have to give me the ring tonight. Tomorrow will be fine."

"I'm coming by tonight, Anna May," he said in a stubborn tone.

"Fine. See you tonight," she replied reaching for the door. She paused when he touched her arm.

"One more thing," he said in a tone she'd heard only once. It was the same deep, sexy tone of voice he'd used when he'd whispered her name the morning after the ice storm.

"What?" she asked as shivers danced down her spine.

"This," he murmured as he leaned across the seat, placing his fingers under her chin. His kiss was soft and gentle and it ended much too soon. "I'll see you tonight," he said.

Anna May didn't remember getting out of the car, but for the rest of the day, she remembered their first kiss.

Chapter Five

Anna May knew she was in trouble when she saw not one but three rental cars parked in front of her house as she turned into her driveway that night. Her parents had wasted no time coming to Atlanta. She'd expected them to come down—just not this soon—and she certainly hadn't expected her brothers.

As the garage door lowered, her mother greeted her at the door. For the first time in five years, she wondered if giving her parents a key to her home was a good idea.

"Hi, Mama." Anna May picked up her briefcase and closed the car door.

With arms open wide, her mother met her in front of her car, enveloping her in a warm embrace. "How's my baby girl?"

Her mother was an inch shorter than her height of five feet six inches. Her black hair was peppered with strands of gray, and her once smooth light brown skin had faint laugh lines around her dark brown eyes.

"I'm fine," she said giving her mother a hug. "When did you guys get in?"

"This afternoon around one o'clock. We called your office, but you were out."

She'd been making wedding plans with Ric. "Oh, I had a few errands to run." Anna May straightened the straps of her purse as they entered her home.

Her father and oldest brother, Steven, stood in the kitchen side by side like matching bookends. Both wore what she'd laughingly referred to as their "preacher garb," black suit, pristine white shirt, and a dark tie. She wanted to make a comment about it, but she had a feeling neither her father nor her brother were in the mood for jokes.

"Hello, Anna May," her father said.

She sighed inwardly at his serious tone, regretting the fact he hadn't called her by her nickname "baby girl," like her mother had.

"Hi, Daddy. Hi, Steve," she said with a sad smile.

"Is she here yet?" The younger of her two brothers walked into the room, his denim shirt and worn blue jeans were as different from his father and brother as his own personality. James, who was two years older than she, had been the object of many arguments in the past. Her parents said they were too much alike to really get along. He stood beside his father—the three men in her family wore the exact same I'm-gonna-get-to-the-bottom-of-this expression.

"What is this I hear about you getting married in a couple of weeks, shorty?" James folded his arms across his chest, his legs planted shoulder width apart. It was a pose guaranteed to put her on the defensive.

She flashed her brother an irritated look. "Do you mind if I change clothes before we have this conversation?" she said heavy with sarcasm.

"No, honey," her mother interjected giving her son a look of warning. "You go ahead and get comfortable, and I'll fix you a plate."

She could hear her father reading James the riot act as she left the kitchen. Placing her briefcase beside a chair in the living room, she prepared herself for the battle to come. I'm not giving in, she said to herself as she walked up the stairs to her bedroom. *I'm getting married and having Ric's child, and there's isn't a thing they can say or do that'll make me change my mind.* With that in mind, she walked into her bedroom wishing she had a suit of armor in her closet.

A suit of armor wasn't what she needed, she thought an hour later. A bomb shelter was more like it.

"You need to think this over," her father said.

"Marriage is such a commitment, baby girl—are you sure you want to do this?" her mother asked.

It was as if her kitchen had been transformed into an arena, and she'd entered a tag team wrestling contest without a partner.

"When did you start dating Ric, and why didn't you say anything when I was here a week ago?" James questioned.

"What's going on? This is too crazy even for you," Steven demanded.

Anna May felt pressure build between her eyes, a sure sign of a whopper of a headache in the making. "No, Daddy. I don't need to think this over. Mom, I know marriage is a commitment and I'm sure I want to do this. James, I don't tell you everything like you don't tell me everything. And Steven, I'm getting married is what's going on." She closed her eyes and pinched the bridge of her nose.

"Anna May," her mother said. "What's going on,

really? This isn't like you to make a major decision like marriage without involving us. Is there something we should know?"

Now was the time to tell them, she thought. Drawing a deep, calming breath, she responded. "I know this is a surprise to you," she continued despite James's snort. "But there are reasons we want to get married this quickly. I've seen several doctors in the past month. I'm fine," she added quickly noting her father's concerned frown. "The tumors are back, and the doctors have advised me to have children now or not have children at all."

Silence filled the room as her family mulled over what she'd said. The confusion that was present in her father's expression was replaced by concern.

"So you're getting married to have children?" her father asked. At her nod yes, he continued. "Ric knows your reason for marrying him?"

"Yes, I was up front with him when I asked him to marry me."

"Wait a minute, you proposed to him?" Steve asked, his brows raised in surprise.

"And asked him to father my child."

"This is crazy, Anna May. You're planning to marry a man you don't love *and* have his child." James rubbed his hand across the nape of his neck. "You might as well hire a divorce lawyer right now."

"We've signed a prenuptial agreement already."

"I know you love Ric, but can you handle being married to a man who's not totally devoted to you? Can you live with him day after day knowing one day your marriage will be over? Can you raise his child alone? Can you do that, baby girl?" Her mother's eyes were bright with tears.

Each question was like an emotional blow to her heart.

Although she'd asked herself those same questions months ago, it still hurt to hear them come from someone else. "I'll have to, Mama," she said quietly.

"This is still the wrong way to start a marriage," Steve said.

"I know that, but I don't have a choice."

"You love him, but I haven't heard you say he loves you," James said as leaned forward in his chair.

She looked at her hands, which she'd folded in her lap and said softly, "He cares for me, and right now that will have to be enough."

Ric parked his car in front of Anna May's house, letting the engine idle. Three additional cars were parked in her driveway. He felt a flash of annoyance and considered coming back when the cars were gone, but he'd said he'd give her the ring tonight, and now was just as good a time as any. With a flick of his wrist, he turned off the engine and stepped out of his car.

The crisp, cold wind had him turning up the collar of his coat. He checked his coat pocket. Through the heavy leather gloves, he felt the square ring box which he'd picked up earlier this evening. As he walked toward her house dodging patches of ice, he wondered if he was doing the right thing by marrying her. It was a question he'd asked himself over and over within the past twenty-four hours. He knew she would love their child and never abandon it like his mother had abandoned him. What he didn't know was if he could be just a friend after they'd become lovers. He'd always held back a part of himself from his previous lovers—but with Anna May, he couldn't. She already knew him better than anyone else, and when it came down to it, he didn't think he wanted to hold anything back with her.

All afternoon images of the two of them making love had kept his temper on edge. Memories of their first kiss had his mind drifting during his two o'clock meeting. The sweet, innocent taste of her lips was like a potent wine in his blood that had him waiting and wanting more.

Ringing the doorbell, he tried to push aside the erotic images in his head. When she opened the door, every erotic image and then some raced through his mind. The hot pink sweater which molded the curves of her breasts was made of a soft knit material that made his fingers ache to find out if it was as soft as it looked. Her jeans were old, almost nearly white with wear. His gaze traveled down her long legs to her bare feet. Damn, he thought, even her feet are sexy.

"Hi," she said giving him a hesitant smile then lowering her voice. "My family's here."

Her family. That explained the cars out front. It also explained the tense air around her.

"Is everything all right?" he asked as he stepped inside, his protective instincts kicked into gear.

Her laugh was sad and mocking. "Not really, but we'll work through it."

Ric tightened his jaw in anger. "Did they give you a hard time?"

"Not really. They're reacting like I thought they would. I'd probably act the same way if one of my brothers suddenly announced he was getting married in a few weeks. They're in the kitchen." She turned in the direction of the kitchen.

"Wait," he said taking off his gloves and placing them on the table at his side. He reached inside his pocket, removing the black velvet jewelry box. The box joined the gloves on the table. Taking her hand, he put the ring on her finger. "Now it's official," he said.

"It's official." She gently stroked the diamond with the tips of her fingers.

Emotions he didn't care to acknowledge flowed through him. He cleared his throat and buried his feelings. "Let's go see your family."

Tension was in the air, hovering over the room like the early morning fog. It reminded him of the days he'd lived with his grandmother when a harsh word or a quick blow was the norm. The four members of the Robinson family looked at him with emotions ranging from surprise from her parents to outright antagonism from both of her brothers.

Instinctively he stood in front of her, creating a protective barrier between Anna May and her family. He could count the number of times he'd seen her parents in the past five years on two fingers, and both times had been accidental. He'd made a point of staying away when her family came into town.

"Mama, Daddy, you remember Ric," she said moving from behind him to stand at his side.

He wanted to thrust her behind him, to shield her from what weapons her family would send her way. Stepping forward, he held out his hand to her father, who was seated at the table. "Mr. Robinson. Mrs. Robinson," he said nodding his head to her mother who sat beside her husband.

"Would you like something to drink?" Anna May asked.

"No. I don't think your family considers this a

social call,'' he said deciding that the best defense was a good offense.

"You got that right," James muttered from his seat at the table.

"Let's put the cards on the table. Anna May and I *are* getting married. None of you are happy with our decision, and you want us to wait. We aren't. We've made our decision, and whether you like it or not we will be married."

"Ric!" She gasped at the steel-like quality of his tone.

His tone softened, and his fiery gaze became gentle as he looked at her. "They need to understand our position on this matter. I won't have them upsetting you again."

"You won't have us upsetting her," James said softly as he came to his feet. "Since when do you have the right to tell us anything, Ice Man?"

Ric met his angry gaze with cool determination. "Anna May gave me the right when she agreed to be my wife."

"Sit down, James," her father said in a forceful tone. When his son was seated, he turned to look at Ric.

Standing his ground, Ric returned the older man's piercing gaze.

"I love my daughter, Ric. Can you say the same?"

The old man had him, Ric thought. Love, hell, he wasn't sure he even knew what the word meant anymore. He cared for Anna May but love her? "No, I can't."

If looks could kill, he'd have been dead twice over, he thought judging from the glares her brothers sent his way.

"Daddy"—Anna May's tearful voice broke the silence—"why?"

"Why?" her father's voice boomed. "I've watched you give your friendship, give your love to him and get very little in return. Now you want to give yourself, become one with a man who can't tell you he loves you? It's time you got something back. You deserve more."

"Yes, she deserves more," Ric said sharply meeting the older man's angry gaze. "But she wants to marry me, and I'm going to see to it that she gets what she wants." He understood her father's anger—however, it wasn't going to stop him from marrying Anna May.

"This is what I want, Daddy."

He looked at his daughter with love, anger, and frustration. "What about what you need?"

"What I want will have to be enough because I'm going to marry him."

Ric felt anger bubble up inside him at the sound of the hurt in her voice. Instinctively he reached for her hand, rubbing his thumb across the back of it to comfort her.

Her father studied their joined hands. "I'm not happy about this marriage," he said. "I think the reasons behind it are wrong, and the two of you are asking for heartache down the road. But if you're determined to get married, all of us will attend the wedding and *all* of us will accept your decision. Right or wrong."

Her father and brothers left early the next morning, and with their departure most of the tension dissipated. She could understand, even sympathize, with their feelings, but she didn't think they understood hers. From the moment she'd learned of her condition, she'd felt as if she were racing against the clock. Time was something she didn't have if she was ever to have a child.

The rattle of dishes interrupted her thoughts. Her mother entered the den, carrying a serving tray with two cups. "I made some hot chocolate," she said placing the tray on the coffee table.

The aroma of her mother's made-from-scratch hot chocolate filled the room. Sitting next to her on the sofa, her mother gave her a cup. They drank the hot chocolate in a comfortable silence.

"Now that your father and brothers are gone, we can talk in peace." Her mother put aside her cup.

"Mama, we've been through this before."

"I know, but I have something I want to say . . . then we won't talk about it again. Okay?"

"Okay."

"I've been thinking about this most of the night. I know your father wouldn't understand what I'm about to tell you, but I think you should know how I feel. Anna May, I think if I were in your situation I'd do exactly what you're doing."

"Really, Mama?"

"Yes, I would. Steve and your father would say remember the trouble Sarah caused when she acted on her own instead of waiting for God to bless her with Isaac, but I don't know if I could just wait around and not do anything." She took her daughter's hand. "Baby girl, you've never hidden the fact that you want children and lots of them. If getting married to Ric makes you happy, then I'm all for it."

Anna May placed her cup on the tray and put her arms around her mother. "Thank you, Mama."

"You're welcome," she said tightening her arms

around her briefly before leaning back and reaching into the pocket of her dress. "Here's a tissue."

She laughed and wiped away the tears on her cheeks. "You're also prepared."

"If you didn't need it, I certainly did," her mother replied wiping away her own tears. "Come on, let's get a move on," she said as she stood.

"Where are we going, Mama?"

"We've got a wedding to plan. Why do you think I'm staying until next week?"

"But I've got everything planned already. I've got my dress, the church is reserved, we've made reservations at a restaurant downtown for the reception, and the invitations have been mailed. There's nothing else to do but show up."

"What about flowers, music, the photographer?"

"The florist will deliver them the day of the wedding. Oh, I'd better make sure Ric tells his aunt and uncle to get there a little early so they can get their flowers."

"You haven't talked to them yourself?"

"No, Ric is taking care of them."

"Uhh, honey. No disrespect to Ric, but when it comes to weddings, men have a tendency to forget things. You might want to talk to them yourself, just to make sure."

"You think so?"

"Trust me on this one."

Later that afternoon when her mother left to run an errand, Anna May called Ric's family after looking up the telephone number in the local telephone directory.

"Hello, Mrs. Steward. This is Anna May Robinson."

"Well, hello, Anna May. Nice to hear from you. It's

been a long time. How's your family?'' Mrs. Steward asked.

Anna May caught her up on her family since the last time they'd spoken to each other years ago.

"Listen, the reason I'm calling," Anna May said, "is that I wanted to make sure you came to the wedding early."

"Oh, you're getting married, dear. Congratulations. Who's the lucky young man?"

Anna May couldn't believe what she was hearing. "Mrs. Steward, Ric and I are getting married. Didn't he tell you?"

"No, he didn't," she said softly, unable to hide the hurt in her voice.

"Well, I'm sure he'll be calling soon. We just became engaged," Anna May hurriedly explained. "You should get your invitation in the mail soon, but let me give you the date and time."

Minutes later she replayed the conversation with his aunt over in her mind. Anna May still couldn't believe that he hadn't told them about the wedding. She was definitely going to talk to him about it. With the verbal invitation issued, she walked to the den where she had extra wedding invitations. She sat down at her desk and addressed an invitation to his family.

Ric and Anna May had played telephone tag the past week because he'd had to go out of the country on business. She'd left him a message stating that the church was booked for the following Saturday. He'd left a message stating he'd had keys to his house made and she should receive them in the mail the next day. She left a message she'd received the keys. He left a message that he'd be back home the next day.

She still hadn't spoken to him about his aunt and uncle. The situation with his family she felt should be discussed face-to-face, not over the telephone. Tonight she'd make sure to talk to him when he arrived home.

It wasn't the most romantic engagement she'd dreamed of: with the candlelight dinners, long sexy telephone conversations, joyous support from both families, and a fiancé eager to make her his wife. No, this engagement was all business, with a prenuptial agreement to prove it.

She should be happy that he even agreed to marry her and give her a child in the first place, she told herself. But deep in her heart, she wanted Ric to love her like she loved him. Mind, body, and soul. She wanted Ric to *want* to marry, to *want* her to have his child.

"Earth to Anna May. Earth to Anna May. Come in, Anna May," Janet said waving her hand in front of Anna May's face.

"Sorry."

"What were you thinking about?" Janet asked. "You were in another world."

"I was thinking about my wedding. It's not like I'd pictured it to be."

"Oh, you mean with the long white dress, a church full of friends and family, and the wedding march playing in the background." Janet placed another stack of clothes in the box she was packing.

"A man who loves me," Anna May said quietly.

"Many women have that kind of wedding and end up divorced. Look at Marianne. She was married in front of three hundred people, in a great big old church to a man who supposedly loved her and look what happened."

"I know," she said then laughed. "This must be prewedding nerves. Ric is the most solid man I know and my best friend."

"Solid isn't the word. Try immovable object."

"He is not, Janet. You need to stop."

"With everybody but *you*, Ric makes Stone Mountain look like a marshmallow. Listen, I've been reading up on this marriage thing," Janet said.

"Oh, no."

"I'm serious now, Anna May. Most couples who've been married twenty, thirty, forty years are friends first and always."

Anna May folded her arms. "Yeah, so?"

"You and Ric are friends. It shouldn't take much for friendship to turn to love."

"How exactly am I supposed to do that? We've been friends for years, and he hasn't fallen in love with me."

"Have you ever let him know you're interested in more than friendship—and I'm not talking about the one time in college when you got drunk because that doesn't count. Everybody at that party thought you were kidding around. I'm talking recent history."

"You know I haven't."

"Well, you'll be living and sleeping with the man you love. If I were you, I'd find a way to make this man fall in love with me."

Could she do it? Could Ric fall in love with her and make their marriage a real marriage? She could give it a try. After all, what did she have to lose.

"You know, Janet, you're right."

"Of course, I'm right."

"And modest, too."

"Modesty is for sissies."

"I thought you said tact was for sissies."

"It is. That's why I can't wait to tell that snotnose apartment manager what he can do with that apartment."

Anna May closed the flaps of the cardboard box. "Are you sure you don't mind moving in?" she asked.

"Anna May. You've asked me twice if I *mind* moving into your house rent free for a year, and I'll tell you again. I don't mind." Janet looked at her friend in disbelief as she assembled and taped another box.

"I know, but I just want to make sure," she said looking around her bedroom. The contents of her nightstand and dresser drawers were now packed away in boxes waiting to be delivered to her new home, Ric's home.

"Hey, girlfriend. I think this wedding is starting to get to you. Are you having premarital jitters?"

"No, I'm fine," Anna May insisted.

"Yeah, right. Then tell me why did you just pack the tape dispenser?"

Heat rushed to her face as she removed the dispenser from the box she'd been packing. "Maybe this wedding thing is starting to get to me."

"You need to take a break," Janet said. "I'll finish in here. You go to a movie, get a facial, do something to take your mind off this wedding for an hour or so. Go to the lingerie place because if this"—she held up a part of white cotton long johns—"is what you're wearing, you need a wardrobe change. Fast."

"Put that back," Anna May said knowing her face was red.

"Oh, wait. Tell me you have sexy lingerie."

"Janet, leave me alone."

"No, no? Silky lingerie is up there with life, liberty, and the pursuit of happiness."

"Last time I checked, silky wasn't mentioned in the Bill of Rights."

"Anna May," her mother called from the front of the house. "Ric's here."

Anna May nearly sighed in relief.

"Hmm," Janet said with a smirk on her face, her eyebrows moving up and down. "Why don't you ask your future husband if silky bits of lingerie should be added to the bill."

"You are a nut."

"No, I'm a woman who appreciates a good-looking man when she sees one, and here's one right now."

What was it about him that made her love him? The sight of him wearing the gray pinstripe suit shouldn't have sent warm, tingly flutters to her stomach. But it did. His smile shouldn't have made her heartbeat race. But it did.

"Hello, Anna May, Janet."

"Hi, Ric," Janet said looking from one to the other before placing the empty box on the floor. "I'm going to get something to drink," she added then left the room.

"I see you've almost finished packing," he said.

"Uh-huh . . ."

"All that's left is the ceremony."

"Yeah . . ."

"What? Are you having second thoughts?"

Anna May sat on the bare mattress. "Second, third, and fourth thoughts. I want a child so much, and I wonder if I didn't strong-arm you into this marriage."

He walked over to the bed and sat beside her. "Nobody strong-arms me. I make my own decisions, and I have decided to marry you."

"I know, but I still feel as if I pushed you into this."

"You couldn't push me if you tried." He sat up

straight, shoulders back and chest out. "I'm tough. I'm the man. I can handle you, woman," he said with a smirk on his face.

"You can handle me? You can handle me!" She had him flat on his back in seconds. Kneeling on the mattress beside his prone body with his tie in her hand, she added, "No, babe. You handle meat. You handle a basketball. You don't handle me."

"Let go of my tie."

"No. Not until you say 'I do not handle Anna May.'"

She saw a mischievous gleam appear in his eyes before her world was turned upside down, and it was she who was flat on her back.

"I don't believe I can say that in all honesty. It seems to me that I handle you quite well."

"That's what you think." She placed her hand beneath his jacket, then ran her fingers along his side, smiling in satisfaction when he jerked away from her tormenting hands. "It's rough being ticklish, isn't it, tough guy?"

"That's it. You've done it now."

Despite her speed and sometimes sneaky tactics she'd learned from wrestling with her brothers, his strength was too much for her. The sound of their harsh breathing filled the room. Her hands were held firmly beside her head. She could feel the mattress with the backs of her hands. His chest leaning slightly against hers. The teasing atmosphere which had surrounded them earlier gave way to a more serious mood as they became aware of their position and each other.

Her heart, racing from their impromptu wrestling match, kicked into high gear as he lowered his head. Her lips parted with anticipation and her eyes closed.

His kiss was like the warm spring sun after a long, cold winter. He teased her lips, softly brushing and stroking until everything around her faded away except him. She felt need rushing through her body, sharp and relentless. The feeling grew stronger as his kisses became more demanding.

"Anna May?" The sound of her mother's voice broke through the sensuous wave of emotions like a bucket of cold water.

Ric straightened and sat on the side of the bed.

"Yes, ma'am," she replied taking Ric's outstretched hand and sitting up as her mother's footsteps became louder.

"Anna May, where's the . . ." Her mother's voice trailed off when she walked into the room. Her gaze traveled from one to the other, then a knowing smile appeared on her face. "Nice shade of lipstick, Ric."

Chapter Six

Long after he'd left Anna May's house, Ric stared into the darkness of the night out of the window of his den, listening to the harsh growl of the wind. His control was slipping. Control, he was beginning to realize, was the one thing that he couldn't afford to lose around Anna May.

Who knew what would have happened between them today if her mother hadn't interrupted when she did? He would have liked to believe that he would've remained in control of the situation, but he wasn't so sure. He wanted Anna May, and from the way she'd responded to him, she wanted him in return.

If this mutual attraction had occurred with another woman, he would have approached the situation like he had in the past and arranged to have a discreet affair if the woman was willing. But he'd make it clear from the beginning that an affair was as far as the relationship would go. Up until last summer this arrangement had worked. Last summer, when he'd realized that his longtime friend, buddy, pal—Anna May—was a desirable and sexy woman. From then on, no other woman had appealed to him. Not that he hadn't dated, he had. But when it came time to develop a deeper relationship, he hadn't been tempted to take the next step. He wanted Anna May, and he couldn't let himself have her.

A phase he'd called it at the time, but his desire for her wasn't showing any sign of diminishing. The kiss they'd shared today aroused lust and passion. It shouldn't have. Hell, she wasn't even dressed for seduction. In her old sweater and corduroy pants, she reminded him of the Anna May of his college years. Young, impulsive, and looking at the world through rose-colored glasses. She was not the type of woman who usually attracted his attention.

Not only had she aroused his desire but feelings that he'd never shared with another woman. Tenderness and possessiveness. And all from the taste of her lips. What was he going to feel when they made love?

That was his problem, he thought. He wasn't going to make love to her. They were going to have sex, share a mutual release of sexual tension to produce the child she wanted. By the time their child was born, he would have gotten over this phase. He and Anna May would hopefully still be friends, and the two of them could go back to their lives with no complications.

But even as the thought crossed his mind, a little voice inside him kept saying, "It's not going to work that way."

Heavy gray clouds hovered over the city, obscuring the view of the Atlanta skyline. Occasionally the weak

winter sun would peek through a break in the clouds.
Pedestrians dressed in heavy wool coats rushed to
their destinations, battling with the wind tunnel effect
created by the towering buildings around them.

Ric noticed none of these things as he prepared
to see his younger brother for the first time. As he
read the report, he wondered if his brother even
knew he existed. Knowing his mother and stepfather,
he seriously doubted it.

"Mr. Justice, Warren's here to see you," his secretary announced crisply.

"Thank you, Mrs. Jones. Send him in."

"I hear congratulations are in order." Warren Morgan walked into Ric's office, closing the door behind
him.

Ric continued to look over the report in front of
him and replied, "Oh?"

Sitting in the leather chair on the other side of
Ric's desk, Warren studied his boss, careful to keep
his curiosity in check. "The word is you've changed
the beneficiary on several of your benefits. Adding
your future wife's name."

"It seems personal information is reported freely
in this company," Ric responded with a hint of steel
in his voice.

Warren smiling inwardly at Ric's response. It was
exactly what he expected. "No. Human resources is
in my department, and I get the information. So
when's the day?"

"Tomorrow—and I'd appreciate it if you'd keep
this to yourself. Anna May wants to keep the ceremony
restricted to family and close friends."

"You got it. So what do you think of Wilson and
Wilson?" he asked noticing the report on his desk.

Closing the report, Ric leaned back in his chair.

"I think I'll wait to hear Wilson's pitch before I make up my mind."

Warren raised a brow in surprise. Usually Ric made his decisions well in advance. Presentations were almost always a formality and rarely had one changed his mind. "Were the reports incomplete?" he asked.

"No, the reports were in-depth. I want to see how Adam Wilson operates in person." He wanted to see how his little brother turned out. Was he a cold bastard like his father? No report could give him that information.

"Why is Adam Wilson any different? Is there something I should know about him?"

"Wilson isn't any different from any other owner on the brink of financial ruin."

"Then why the change?"

"Morgan, change is sometimes good. It keeps everyone guessing."

"Are you trying to keep Wilson guessing?"

The intercom buzzed, and Mrs. Jones announced Adam Wilson's arrival.

Although he hadn't seen his brother in years, he would have recognized Adam Wilson as his brother among hundreds of strangers on the street. His mother's features were prominent in his brother from his mocha brown skin, high and sharply defined cheeks, to the dimple in his chin which appeared when he smiled. Like he did now.

"Mr. Justice, I'm Adam Wilson."

Ric walked from around his desk and shook his brother's hand. They stood eye to eye. He thought he saw a flicker of recognition in his brown eyes. Eyes the same shade as his own. Adam had been a baby when they'd last seen each other. There was no way he would know him.

"Good to meet you, Mr. Wilson. This is Warren Morgan, my business manager."

"Mr. Morgan," Adam said offering his hand.

"Shall we begin?" Ric gestured toward the conference table.

Risk taker was the impression Ric developed of Adam Wilson as he listened to his presentation. The business plan he'd developed was solid, well researched, and a calculated risk. It was the type of plan Ric had devised many times in his career.

"You have a good plan for Wilson and Wilson," Ric said when Adam asked for questions. "However, what's to keep your company from experiencing the same problems later on?"

"It's no secret that Wilson and Wilson is in a financial bind," Adam responded meeting Ric's gaze with a determined gaze of his own. "Our equipment is outdated, and the company hasn't changed as the market has changed. I've reorganized my company to reflect the change in market. In addition . . ."

He was good, very good, Ric thought as Adam explained the changes he'd made at Wilson and Wilson. Unlike some who thought they could hide their company's problems, Adam brought them out in the open and disclosed his solutions.

An hour later when Adam Wilson left, Ric and Warren sat at the conference table.

"There's no doubt about it. Wilson will turn his company around if he's given enough time," Warren said.

"Yes, but would an outright buyout be profitable for the company rather than two-year financing?"

"Either way the company would make money, but I got the feeling that Wilson is attached to the company."

"We'll deal with that should the situation arise. I want to see if the deal with the city of Atlanta comes through for him."

"You want to keep him waiting that long?"

"He doesn't have another offer on the table. We can wait."

"Okay. You know if I didn't know you were an only child, I'd swear you two were related."

Ric raised a single brow. "Oh?"

"It would be funny for you to suddenly have a wife and a brother."

"Yes, that would be funny," Ric replied being careful to keep his face expressionless.

With a shake of his head, Warren rose from his chair. "I'll keep you posted on Wilson. Oh, and congratulations on your upcoming marriage." With that he left Ric's office.

Ric rose and walked to the large windows behind his desk. Gray clouds raced across the sky. The tops of the buildings were hidden beneath them.

Control. Finally he had the upper hand, not his stepfather. He had the power and control to save or destroy the business Evan Wilson had built. The urge was strong within him to systematically destroy Wilson and Wilson. If Adam Wilson had been like his father, Ric wouldn't have hesitated to do just that, but his gut feeling told him Adam was different from his father.

He'd give Adam a chance to prove himself like he would any other businessman. Judge him on his own merit, not for the sins of his father. As he watched the clouds move across the sky, he wondered if anyone else would notice the family resemblance between him and Adam. He was definitely going to make sure Anna May didn't get wind of it. Her soft heart would try to make a Kodak moment between them. Make them a family. He definitely didn't need family.

Evan Wilson wielded his power the old-fashioned way, through intimidation. Which was why he was able to bully his way past his son's temporary secretary and into his old office. Adam had transferred his old secretary when he caught her giving him confidential files a month ago.

Adam had agreed to take over Wilson and Wilson only if he took early retirement and resigned as president. Evan had balked at first. *He'd* run the company for thirty years. *He* was the one to build the company from the ground up. His father had been content to stay a small-sized company, but it was he who had expanded and made it one of the most powerful black-owned companies in the Southeast. And his son wanted him totally out of the day-to-day operations of Wilson and Wilson before he'd consider joining the company.

The only reason he'd agreed to step down as president was that he was sure his son would see the error of his ways and beg him to come back. He was a reasonable man, and he wouldn't let his own son beg for his help for long.

But Adam hadn't begged him to come back in the nine months since he'd left. In fact, he had all but threatened to have him barred from entering the doors of the company if he caught him in his office again. Evan smiled to himself as he sat behind the desk that was once his, savoring the power and control that came with the title of owner. He had made and destroyed men's careers with a single telephone call. It was that kind of power that he missed the most.

With the desk key he had duplicated before giving the original to Adam, Evan unlocked the old maple desk. Taking his time, he removed several folders. He'd had his former secretary get a copy of Adam's schedule for the day, and he knew Adam was to be in a meeting out of the building for several hours. He would have felt better if he knew exactly where Adam went, but Adam's new secretary had no idea where the meeting was to take place.

Looking over the balance sheet, Evan smiled in satisfaction. His boy was making money but not enough to make up for the last few years of debt the company had acquired. He could have told him not to upgrade the equipment, and he would have definitely *not* given the employees a raise when the company was losing money.

Lucky. His boy was lucky, Evan thought as he flipped through the pages in the folder. Luck could get you only so far in business. The past few years had been hard on the company's bottom line, but he'd worked his way out of the red in the past, and he was sure he could do it in the future.

He glanced at page after page of financial data. Soon his son would come to him for help. Soon he would be in power once more. His smile crumpled when he came to the last page. His blood ran cold, then a chilling rage enveloped him as he read and reread the words on the page.

There was no way in hell he would let his company be bought out by the Justice Company. He'd burn it to the ground, like he'd done years ago, before he allowed anyone—especially Trevor Justice's bastard—to get his hands on Wilson and Wilson. Taking the page out of the folder, he slowly and methodically began tearing the page into tiny pieces.

Adam Wilson came to an abrupt stop when he saw his father sitting behind his desk. "What are you doing here, Dad?"

"It seems as if I didn't get here fast enough," he said sarcastically. "What the hell are you doing even talking with people at the Justice Company?"

"What I do with the company doesn't concern you anymore. I bought you out," Adam said sternly as he walked into his office.

"If you think I'm going to let my own son sell out to a Justice, you can think again," Evan yelled.

"The company doesn't belong to you. It belongs to me, and I will do what I think is best. You don't have any say in the way the company is run. You gave up that right when you retired."

His father rose from the chair, his eyes narrowed with rage. "I won't let you sell my company to Ric Justice. I'll destroy this place with my bare hands first."

Adam kept his expression blank. He'd learned over the years that it was best to keep a cool head when dealing with his father. "What has he done to you?"

"He's a low-class, do-nothing bastard like his father was before him."

Adam laughed mockingly. "That 'do nothing' is worth hundreds of millions."

Evan slammed his hand on the desk. "I'd rather go bankrupt than to see a Justice with any part of Wilson and Wilson."

"You mean you would put all of our employees on the street before getting help from the Justice Company? Is keeping your pride intact worth the livelihood of thousands of families?"

"Look, boy. I'm telling you—don't have anything to do with him."

"And I'm telling you I'll do whatever it takes to make this company profitable. Even deal with the Justice Company." Adam walked to the door and held it open. "Now, Dad, it's time for you to leave." His tone was unyielding and determined.

Blood rushed to his father's face. With his jaw clenched, Evan Wilson stalked to the door. "I'm warning you, Adam. I don't want you even talking to the Justice Company."

Adam met the fiery brown gaze of his father with a determined one of his own. "Goodbye, Dad."

His father marched out of the office. Adam closed the door quietly behind him before walking to his desk. Four manila folders lay open on top of the desk. He put his briefcase on top of the desk, then quickly scanned the contents of the folders.

Surface information, he thought, as he gathered the papers, strictly surface information. Important documents were stored in the newly installed safe in the wall behind his desk. He and the security managers were the only people in the company who knew of the safe's existence. A few months after his retirement, his father had shown his inability to voluntarily stay out of the company. The safe was just one of the precautionary measures Adam had taken to ensure that his father couldn't get his hands on the wrong information.

Adam sat in the chair and opened his briefcase. The presentation he'd prepared for Ric Justice was on top of the pile. His company's financial situation had been disclosed in great detail during the hour-long meeting. Ric Justice kept his opinion of the plan he'd presented to himself. He understood how Ric got the name Ice Man. His control and the icy edge of his voice made him feel as if he'd been thrust into the frozen tundra of Alaska with only a suit jacket for protection.

But he could handle whatever the Ice Man dished out as long as he invested in his company. Hiding the fact that his company needed capital was an impossibility, but with the proposed improvements he and his employees had come up with, Wilson and Wilson would be out of debt in the next year and extremely profitable the following year. All he had to do was convince Ric to invest in his company.

Ric Justice's business savvy wasn't the only reason he'd sought him out. Finding a copy of Ric's birth certificate among his mother's papers had been a shock. He had a brother. A brother he'd never known existed until his mother's death a few months ago.

Why the secrecy? Why hadn't his mother mentioned her other son? Why hadn't his father?

He was curious about Ric Justice. From the articles he'd managed to find about Ric, and the interview he'd had today, Ric seemed to be a pretty decent man. His mother had been a beautiful but flighty woman. She depended on her husband to make most of the decisions. Even so, why would she all but ignore her firstborn? Adam closed his eyes. The question burned in his mind. It was a question he was going to find the answer to.

Her mother was driving her crazy. Anna May pushed the grocery cart down the spice aisle of the Dekalb Farmers' Market. Today, the day before her wedding, her mother decided she wanted to make curried shrimp, Anna May's favorite dish.

"It's not like I'm going to eat any of it," she muttered down the aisle. She was too nervous to eat. This time tomorrow she would be Mrs. Garrick Trevor Justice. Anna May Justice. The last virgin over the age of thirty in the state of Georgia.

As she made her way to the seafood area, doubt began to bubble to the surface. Was she doing the right thing, or was she on a course that would ruin her friendship with Ric? When she reached the seafood counter, a very pregnant woman stood in line in front of her. All of her doubt dissipated at the sight of the woman.

Her resolve crystallized, and she straightened her shoulders. Giving birth to a child, a child created with the man she loved, was worth all the moments of doubts and insecurity she was feeling. It was worth the disagreement with her family. It was worth risking the best friend she'd ever had.

She remembered Janet's advice to make Ric love her. She had to try. Ric's love was worth the risks she was taking. If her gamble paid off, she would have a child to love and a loving husband. Yes, it was worth the risk.

Thirty minutes later she parked inside her garage.

Her mother met her at the door. "Here, let me help you."

"It's only two bags, Mama."

"Well, give me one." Her polite tone was at odds with the commanding way she took the bag out of Anna May's hand.

"Another package came for you while you were out," her mother said.

"Oh, what was it?" Anna May put her bag on the kitchen table.

"I don't know. I left it in the den. Why don't you see what it is. I'll put away the groceries."

She'd heard that tone in her mother's voice before,

and she knew she would have to do what her mother said.

"Yes, ma'am," she replied then walked down the hall to her den. Frowning, she reached for the knob of the door. She never kept this door closed. With a shrug, she turned the knob and walked inside.

"Surprise!" Janet, Marianne, and Raina yelled. Anna May stared in wonder. Her den had been transformed. Balloons and streamers hung from the walls. Her desk was stacked with gaily wrapped gifts, and in the middle of her coffee table was a cake from her favorite bakery in town.

"What is this?" she asked still a little dazed.

"It's a wedding shower, baby girl," her mother replied from behind her.

"You sent me to the farmers' market to get me out of house?"

"Of course, I did. How else were we going to give you a shower?" her mother replied taking her hand and leading her to a chair decorated with balloons. "Now have a seat and enjoy yourself."

"Wait," Marianne said. "We've got to take a picture before everybody else gets here."

"Everybody else?" Anna May asked.

"Yes, the other women at the office and some of the ladies from church. You came back too early for them to get here," Raina answered.

"Come on, ya'll. Gather around Anna May while I set this up." Marianne toyed with the video camera.

As her mother and friends gathered around her, she said a silent prayer of thanks.

Minutes later her den was filled. Twenty women from her church and office wandered around the den, drinking punch and eating finger sandwiches.

"Okay, ladies. It's time for the bride to open her

presents. Anna May, come and have a seat." Janet raised her voice over the muffled noise of the crowd.

Anna May sat down in the balloon-decorated chair. "I really appreciate this," she said.

"You don't have to thank us. I'm sure your husband will thank us enough," said one of the women from her office.

She blushed as the women around her laughed knowingly.

"Here's the first gift," Raina said sitting between her and the desk.

Anna May opened the card. "Oh, it's from Mama." She ripped the paper from the box. The name of a famous lingerie shop was embossed on the box top. Lifting the top, Anna May gasped and Raina starting laughing.

"What? Hold it up so all of us can see," Marianne demanded from behind the video camera.

Reluctantly she held up the virginal white, totally sheer chiffon gown.

"Ooh. She'll have that gown on all of two minutes," another lady added.

"You think it will last that long?" her mother asked.

"Mama," Anna May cried knowing her face was as red as a tomato.

"What? You'll find out what we're talking about tomorrow," her mother responded.

Anna May put the gown back in the box and reached for the next gift, hoping it wouldn't be as risqué as her mother's gift. She was wrong.

"This one is from Marianne," she said after reading the card. Eagerly she opened the box. Laughter erupted when she held up the black lace and satin merry widow and matching thong.

When she could control her laughter, her mother

said, "I wouldn't wear that the first night, baby girl. You might not be ready for his reaction."

Later when the majority of her guests had left and her gifts lay open on the coffee table, Anna May and the other members of the Ladies' Club drank a final cup of coffee.

"Did Mama leave to go to the airport already?"

"Yes. She said she wanted to get there early in case your brother was able to get the earlier flight," Raina replied.

"Well, Anna May, this is it. Your last night as a single woman," Janet said with her stocking-clad feet propped on the table.

"Yes, this is it," she replied wrapping both hands around the cup.

"It's also the last night that your virginity will still be intact. We're your friends," Raina said softly. "And your mother might or might not talk to you about your wedding night, but we don't want you to go in unaware."

"That's really nice, but I know about sex," she replied feeling heat return to her face.

"Knowing and doing are two different things," Marianne added folding her legs beneath her. "That's like reading a book on how to drive and actually driving."

"What we're trying to say is, If you have any questions, ask us—but we figured you'd be too embarrassed to ask us, so the three of us came up with a list of things we wanted to tell you," Janet said.

Anna May listened as each of her friends spoke frankly about the act of making love. At several times during their speech, she put her hands over her flushed cheeks.

"The last thing is only the two of you can decide

what's right or wrong in lovemaking. Talk to Ric. Tell him what you liked or didn't like. Ask him to do the same. You have to work at pleasing each other. It's not something that most people know how to do right off the bat," Marianne said.

"I don't know what to say," Anna May said softly.

"You don't have to say anything. We want you to know that we want this marriage to work just as much as you do. Maybe next time we give you a shower, it'll be a baby shower," Raina said.

"I hope so. I really hope so."

"Are you ready?" her brother, Steven, asked as he entered the church nursery which Anna May and her mother used as a changing area. The music from the church orchestra filled the room and was silenced when he closed the door.

Anna May looked down at the winter white, two-piece suit she'd chosen over the more traditional wedding gown and veil. She turned to the side to check the hem of the floor-length skirt.

"I'm as ready as I'm ever going to be," she said.

"Be happy, baby girl," her mother said giving her a hug before she left the room to take her seat in the church.

The two of them stood alone in the room. "Are you sure this is what you want to do?" he asked.

"I'm sure," she said with conviction.

He offered her his arm and they left the room. Her stomach clenched at the familiar notes of the wedding march. Subconsciously she was aware of the small group, consisting of her friends and family, rising to their feet—but her focus was on the man standing at the end of the aisle.

Lord, the man was handsome, she thought as she walked toward him. He wore a black tuxedo, white shirt, and a black bow tie. Never in her wildest dreams could she imagine him looking as good as he did. She tightened her grasp on Steven's arm. He looked calm and confident as if getting married was something he did every day. While she felt as if a herd of crazed butterflies had taken residence in her stomach.

Steven kissed her cheek when they reached the end of the aisle. Ric smiled and took her hand as they turned to face her father. She repeated the sacred vows to love, honor, and obey until death do us part with all the love she had inside of her. The vows were real to her, and she meant to keep them.

"You may kiss the bride," she heard her father say. Shyly she looked at her husband. Her heartbeat quickened as he lowered his head. The touch of his lips on hers stole her breath. With soft questing stroking of his tongue, he parted her lips. The taste of him made her shiver in delight. Slowly he lifted his head. She opened her eyes and met his dark golden gaze which held promises of things to come.

Dimly she heard the sound of her father's voice. "Friends, I present to you Mr. and Mrs. Garrick Justice." Ric took her hand as they turned to face the audience. His hand tightened on hers almost to the point of being painful. Anna May looked at him, puzzled by his reaction. She then followed his gaze to an older couple sitting in the back of the church.

"What's wrong, Ric?" she asked.

He turned and looked her. Fierce emotions raged in his gaze, and in a cold voice he asked, "Who invited my aunt and uncle?"

Before she could respond, her friends walked up.

"Congratulations," Marianne said giving Anna May a hug. One by one her friends and family offered their best wishes to the couple. She felt Ric stiffen when his aunt and uncle, John and Betty Steward, the last people in the receiving line, approached them. The gray in Mrs. Steward's hair was more pronounced, and Mr. Steward was completely bald on the top, but the couple looked nearly the same as they did the last time she'd seen them years ago at her high school graduation.

"Mr. and Mrs. Steward. It's good to see you again," she said giving them both a hug. The four of them stood alone as guests began to leave the church and make their way to the reception.

"Nice to see you again, Anna May," Mrs. Steward said, her gaze on the silent man standing beside her. "How are you, Ric?" she asked, her voice a little shaky.

"I'm fine Aunt Betty, Uncle John," he said in a coolly emotionless tone.

"We'd love to have the two of you over for dinner sometime," Mrs. Steward added.

"We'd—" Anna May began only to be interrupted by her husband.

"Maybe later," Ric said in a tone which said "probably never." "Excuse me. I need to see if the limousine has arrived."

"Ric," she said as he walked away.

"Let him go, child," Mrs. Steward said with tears in her eyes.

"I'm so sorry, Mrs. Steward."

"It's not your fault," Mr. Steward said. "Ric has never stayed around us any longer than necessary."

"But you're his family."

"I'm sure you know family doesn't mean much to

Ric. After what his mother and grandmother did to him, I'm surprised he can stand to be around us at all," Mrs. Steward said dabbing the tears from her eyes with a handkerchief.

"He rarely talks about them. I know his mother sent him to live with his grandmother when he was little, then he came to live with you when he was fourteen. What happened to him?" Anna May asked wanting to know the answer but feeling a sense of dread like she was about to open Pandora's box.

"We don't know all of it, but Ric's mother remarried, and her husband didn't want him around after his son was born. He had her send Ric to live with her mother. His grandmother was a cruel woman. When we came back from overseas, we went to visit him." She paused to wipe away her tears. "The way she treated him—like he was nothing. I couldn't let my brother's child live like that, so John and I filed for custody of him. For the first month he lived with us, he never came within arm's length of either of us."

"We think his grandmother beat him," Mr. Steward said.

"What?" Anna May asked in shock. "He never told me."

Mrs. Steward continued, "He never did tell us either. I think by the time we came into his life when he was fourteen, Ric couldn't trust anyone. Except maybe you."

"Come on, Anna May," James called from the rear of the church. "Your car and husband are waiting. And I'm hungry, so get a move on."

Mrs. Steward took her hand then said, "Love him. He needs somebody to love him."

Anna May put her hand over Mrs. Steward's and squeezed it. "I do love him. With all my heart."

As the trio made their way down the aisle, Anna May felt a mounting sense of dread. She'd asked Ric to give her the one thing that he feared the most.

A family.

"Hey, the bride isn't supposed to be frowning," James said when she reached him. With the pad of his thumb, he brushed the line that had formed between her brows. If only her worries could disappear as quickly.

She smiled at her brother and kissed his cheek. "How's that?"

"Much better," he said and led her out of the church.

Ric stood beside a silver Rolls Royce complete with chauffeur.

James whistled softly. "I have to admit, your husband has style."

Style wasn't the only thing he had, she thought. From the look in his eyes, he was hanging on to his temper by a thread. With her smile firmly in place, she said to her brother, "I'll see you at the reception."

The chauffeur hurried to open the door as they approached the car. Ric held out his hand when she reached his side. She was thankful for his help as she tried to gracefully sit in the car. He sat down beside her on the lush leather seat.

"Are you *really* angry with me?" she asked as the chauffeur walked around the car.

He looked at her, his gaze steady and cold. "We'll talk about this later."

Yup, Anna May thought. He's really mad with me. What a way to start a marriage.

The short ride to the restaurant was made in

silence. She wanted to talk to him about his family, but the sight of his clenched jaw made her change her mind.

The reception was held in old Victorian home which had been recently converted to a restaurant. As she and Ric entered the private dining room, a violinist began to play a romantic tune.

A waiter led them to a large table where most of their party was seated. She avoided her mother's probing gaze as Ric held her chair. At her father's request, dinner was served.

They could have kept mine, she thought later that evening when the waiter removed her nearly full plate. Although both she and Ric were cordial, she could tell that her mother sensed something was wrong. Something *was* wrong. She was afraid she would end up fighting with her husband on her wedding night.

"I'd like to propose a toast," her father said as he stood, holding up his glass of sparkling apple cider. He waited until all of the guests were silent before he began. "To my daughter and her new husband. I pray that God blesses your marriage. I hope you two experience the happiness your mother and I have had over the past forty years," he said smiling at his wife. "I pray He blesses you with children and that His love flows abundantly in your home. To Mr. and Mrs. Garrick Justice."

As family and friends raised their glasses in a toast, Anna May felt the sting of tears in her eyes. Taking a sip from her glass, she hoped her father's prayer would come to pass, but she was afraid it wouldn't.

Chapter Seven

"What was I supposed to do, Ric? *Not* invite them to the wedding when I just invited them to the reception?" Anna May leaned against the foyer wall, slipping off a single white satin pump and rubbing her tired foot.

The ride to Ric's home had been made in virtual silence. Silence which was magnified by the nearly soundproof interior of the limousine and the inky darkness of the night. She'd waited until they were alone before she confronted him.

Ric raised a single brow and replied coolly, "I expected you to let me handle matters."

"If I'd let you handle things, your family wouldn't have been there at all," she said removing her other shoe.

"Exactly," he said.

She put her hands on her hips in frustration, her shoes hanging from her fingers. "Why didn't you tell me you didn't want them to come to our wedding in the first place? If I'd known you didn't get along with your aunt and uncle, I wouldn't have called them."

Ric tugged, leaving the ends of his black bow tie unbound against his crisp white shirt. "I didn't say I didn't get along with them. They don't have a place in my life anymore."

"Ric, they raised you. Why don't they have a place in your life?"

"I've paid my debt to them. I don't owe them anything else," he said walking down the hallway.

Following him around the corner past his living room, she replied, "Paid your debt? They're your family. You don't pay for family."

He paused in front of the stairs. "Leave it alone, Anna May."

"I don't understand," she said gathering her skirt and climbing the stairs beside him. "They seem like a nice couple. Did they mistreat you or something?"

"I imagine they treated me well enough."

"Then why didn't you want your family around?" she asked frustrated by his stubbornness.

He stopped in front of the bedroom she'd used the night of the ice storm. "I guess I'm not the family type. I had your things put in here. If you don't like this room, we can move you to one of the other two bedrooms."

A wave of disappointment washed over her. She'd looked forward to sharing his master bedroom. His master bed was what she really wanted to share. "This is fine," she said.

"Good. I'm going to get out of this suit. See you later." He turned and walked down the hall.

Anna May walked to the bed and sat down, dropping her shoes on the floor. This was not the way she'd pictured their first night together. Things had started going downhill the minute Ric saw his aunt and uncle. No, that wasn't true, she thought to herself, folding her arms. Her relationship with Ric had changed the morning after the ice storm. They'd approached each other like two weary soldiers, each unwilling to totally let down their guard around the other.

Since her hasty proposal, there had been only a few pockets of time where the old, easy friendship had surfaced. And she missed it. She missed being able to talk to him about practically anything. She even missed his dry sense of humor, which she sometimes had a hard time following.

"You've made your bed, now lie in it," she muttered, her voice breaking the silence of the room. With a sigh she looked down at the full-sized bed. Unfortunately it seemed as if the bed she was to lie in wasn't Ric's bed.

The weight of the gold band felt strange, Ric thought, looking down at the object in question. The ring symbolized the vows he'd made before God and man. Vows to love, honor, and cherish his wife.

Anna May.

He'd honored her before their marriage. To love her and to cherish her, he wasn't so sure he could do.

His mother had told him she loved him every time she came to visit. But she never took him home with her, never brought his little brother with her—instead after her visits, he would have another bruise made by the back of his grandmother's heavy hand. The beatings stopped after he moved in with his aunt and uncle. They'd taken care of him for four years, and he'd made sure they were compensated for their effort. The trust he'd set up for them ensured that neither of them ever had to work again. In his opinion he'd more than paid for four years of food, clothing and shelter.

If his grandmother had been alive, she too would have been paid for the eight years she'd taken care of him. It would have given him a great deal of satisfaction to give the old woman a wad of money. He could still remember the numerous times she'd told him he owed her for the food he ate, the roof over his head, and the clothes on his back. He never wanted to owe her or anyone else a thing. When he was old enough, he began to work after school to pay her back. He never did. She'd died a few years before he could completely pay her back.

Anna May had given him her trust and friendship year after year without asking for anything in return. Until now. She'd asked him to give her a child. Not only did she want his child, she wanted to conceive the old-fashioned way. If she'd asked him to donate his sperm, he would have been leery but he would have done it. He would do just about anything for her. The thought of having sex with Anna May made him edgy.

He had a feeling that he couldn't treat having sex with Anna May the same way he'd treated his women in the past. He'd walked away from his relationships in the past without ever looking back. With Anna May he knew that would never be the case.

Twisting the ring around his finger, he wondered if he'd done the right thing. He could have turned her down and knowing her, she would have still treated him as a friend—however, the thought of her making love to another man triggered possessive feelings he hadn't known he felt toward her.

He wanted to be the man who introduced her to the delights of the flesh. He wanted to be the first and only man to watch her as she dissolved into a thousand pieces.

He wanted to feel her legs around his waist. He wanted his seed to grow inside her. He wanted her plain and simple. And it scared the living daylights out of him.

An hour later she wondered how she could have been so down in the dumps. After she'd soaked in a tub filled with jasmine-scented bubbles, her relationship with Ric came into focus. Dressed in a floor-length, white silk gown and matching robe, the most conservative article of clothing she'd received at her bridal shower, she walked down the hall in search of her husband.

So Ric was upset with her, she thought tightening the belt of her robe. This wasn't the first time, she thought, remembering how angry he was this summer when she'd gone rafting down Tallulah Gorge, a valley which had been dried up when the dam had been built miles upstream on the river. For the first time since the dam had been built, the state of Georgia allowed the river to run in the gorge. Rapids with names like Hurricane and Death came to life again. Ric had been livid when she told him about her adventure.

"You could have been killed," he said in a deceptively calm voice.

"I was perfectly safe. The other rafters were professionals."

"How many times have you been white water rafting?"

"I've been once before, and they assured me that it was safe. They were right. I'm here in one piece. It was a once in a lifetime opportunity. I don't think they'll ever release the river again. I couldn't say no when they asked if I wanted to come."

"You're going to get in over your head one day. Didn't you stop to think of the things that could have gone wrong?"

"Yeah, yeah, yeah. Walking across the street is dangerous, but people do it every day."

"It's not the same, and you know it." He frowned at her.

She smiled as she remembered the lecture he'd given her and the hours it had taken her to soothe his anger. The most important thing she'd remembered was no matter how angry he'd been with her, he'd never stopped being her friend. Their marriage, she decided when she reached his bedroom door, wasn't going to end their friendship if she had anything to do with it.

She knocked on the door, then smoothed her hands over her thighs. Nerves, she thought in disgust as she waited for him to answer but receiving none. She knocked again, this time a little harder, listening closely for a sound in the room. Still no answer. Puzzled she walked down the hall. He was somewhere in the house, and she was going to find him. She found him in his office.

He'd changed out of the tuxedo into navy dress pants and a white shirt. The single lamp on his desk worked in vain to dispel the darkness in the room. Ric stood with his back to the door, staring into the darkness of the night. The white fabric of his shirt lay taut across his shoulders. He had a restless quality about him despite his stillness.

"Ric," she called softly.

He turned from the window. "Yes."

"We need to talk," she said as she walked into the room.

"About what?" he asked.

"About us. I don't want our friendship to suffer just because we're married. We've been friends for years, and we've always been able to talk to each other. If you didn't want your family at our wedding, I think you should have told me. I may not have understood, but I would have respected your wishes. You would have talked to me before. I want to know what changed," she said standing beside his desk.

"I've never talked to you about my family. That hasn't changed," he replied.

"So talking about your family is off limits?"

"Yes."

"Fine. We won't talk about your family. Why didn't you tell me earlier?" she asked.

"It didn't seem important at the time," he said from his position beside the window.

"Ric, I don't want to spend another minute feeling like I have the past few hours. I don't want to lose my best friend. If I do something to make you angry, tell me. I'd rather have you yell at me than get the cold, silent Ice Man treatment."

"When did I give you the silent treatment? If I remember correctly, I did tell you I was mad at you for inviting my aunt and uncle to the wedding."

"Yes, you did, but you left angry and that's never happened before. I felt like you dumped me in the guest room and left. Usually you lecture me until you're not mad anymore. Are you still mad at me?" she asked.

"No, I'm not mad at you," he said.

"Good," she said leaning against his desk. "We need to talk about my room."

He frowned. "What's wrong with it?"

"Nothing's wrong with it except I'm in it."

"What?"

"I don't want to stay in that room," she said inwardly wincing at the pouting tone in her voice.

"We'll move your things into another room."

"I don't want another room, I want to be in your room."

"My room?"

"I was hoping it would be our room."

"You want to move into the master bedroom with me," he said as if he were getting his facts straight.

"Ric. We're married. Married people share a bedroom. Besides, how am I supposed to become pregnant if we sleep in separate beds?"

He turned and faced the window before replying. "We'll move your things tonight."

"What's wrong? You don't sound too happy about it."

He turned to her then said, "Nothing's wrong."

Something was definitely wrong.

Ric went to the dressing room door where Anna May had disappeared after muttering, "I'll be just a second." Twenty minutes later the door remained closed.

"Anna May? Are you all right?"

A thump accompanied her muffled voice. "I'm fine. I'll be out in a second."

"You said that fifteen minutes ago," he muttered and walked away. When she'd closed the door twenty minutes ago, he'd gone into action. A bottle of sparkling apple cider on ice sat in a holder beside the bed. Calla lilies adorned her pillow on the bed, a bottle of jasmine-scented body oil warmed in a container of its own, and soft music played on his stereo. Everything was in place, except the bride.

Anna May deserved more than the seductive atmosphere he'd created in his—no, their—bedroom. She deserved the hearts and flowers, the happily ever after. She deserved to have a husband who loved her. Instead, she had him. A man who wasn't sure he could ever love anyone.

He frowned as another thump sounded from the other side of the door. What was she doing in there? He'd assumed that she'd gone in there to change, but how long did it take to put on the gauzy piece of fluff she'd tried to conceal? He turned his attention to the door when he heard the latch release. Standing in the doorway wearing the same white robe she'd worn earlier, was his wife. His very nervous wife, he noted, from the way she tugged at the ends of her belt. If she tightened it any further, she'd create a tourniquet for her waist. He had to get her to relax.

"Would you like something to drink?" he asked putting a small amount of distance between them.

"Er . . . no."

"Sure? I'm having some," he said lifting the bottle out of the ice bucket.

"No."

He poured himself a glass and took a sip, studying her over the glass as she fussed with the knot of her belt.

"Relax, Anna May. We've got all night."

He felt a wave of desire as she bit her bottom lip. "Er . . . if it's all right with you, I'd just as soon get it over with."

He put down the glass and walked to her side. With her head down and her hands twisting her belt, she couldn't have looked more vulnerable and uncertain. Or so utterly appealing. "It doesn't work like that," he said stroking her shoulders.

"It doesn't?" she asked breathlessly.

"No. Sometimes it could take hours." He pulled her toward him and kissed her brow.

"I don't think I can stay in this thing for hours, Ric," she said earnestly taking short quick breaths.

"What thing?"

She stepped back, fumbling with the knot of her belt until it gave way in her hand. "This thing," she said opening her robe.

He'd always considered white to be a virginal color—however, virginal was the last thing that came to mind when he saw the pure white creation she had on. Sheer mesh and lace both revealed and concealed her breasts. He could almost make out the dark brown skin of her nipples beneath the delicate white lace. The sheer material hugged and defined the pouty curves of her breasts, which threatened to spill over with every breath she took. His own oxygen supply seemed to desert him as heat rushed through his body as his gaze traveled down her body.

Satiny white Lycra clung tightly to the curve of her waist before giving way to more lace which barely covered her feminine mound. Two lace garters held lace-topped stockings, leaving the tops of her brown thighs bare and her shapely legs covered with sheer white nylons. Her feet were encased in two strips of white leather with high heels.

"I can't breathe in this thing," she said.

That was funny because he couldn't seem to breathe, either. "You could always take it off," he murmured barely able to say the words.

Her eyes widened in appeal. "I barely got into this thing without killing myself. I don't know why I let Janet talk me into wearing this thing." Her satin robe slipped off her bare shoulders, pooling at her elbows.

His mouth went dry as every nerve ending in his body seemed to relocate to his manhood. "I'll help you."

Uncertainty flashed in her eyes as she studied his face. She was smart to be uncertain, he thought. All he wanted to do was peel her out of her clothes and bury himself inside her. He hadn't felt this way since he was a teenager. But he had to get himself under control. She was a virgin and deserved, no, needed him to be in control.

"The hooks are in the back," she said presenting him with her back, as she removed her robe.

He forgot to breathe.

She was nearly naked from the waist down. A long series of hooks spanned from her shoulders to the small of her back. A thin, white scrap of lace did nothing to hide the twin orbs of her firm brown buttocks. His hands ached to cup and knead them. A bead of sweat slid down his temple. With shaking hands, he tackled the first hook and nearly groaned. Her skin felt soft and warm against his knuckles.

Control. He had to stay in control. He concentrated on hook after hook. Slide and release, slide and release until the two binding panels hung freely at her back. A long red line where the two panels were joined bore witness to her discomfort. He traced the line gently with the tips of his fingers.

Her muscles stiffened.

"Anna May," he said softly.

"Wh . . . what?" she said with her head lowered and her hands pressing the wisps of lace to her chest.

"Do us both a favor and go lay on the bed."

She hesitated for a moment before walking over to the king-sized bed. If she knew how much the sway of her hips and the rise and fall of her buttocks turned him on, he had a feeling she wouldn't have taken so long to walk to his bed. He released his clenched hands and forced himself to relax.

"I'll be right back," he said when she sat on the mattress then walked to the master bath. When he returned, he held two large towels which had been warmed by the heated towel rack. He put them on the bed beside her. Kneeling in front of her, he removed her slippers and placed her foot on his thigh. With shaking hands, he unsnapped the garters and rolled her stocking down her leg before letting the nylon float to the carpet. The other stocking quickly joined its mate. He rose to his feet. Cupping her chin with his hand, he leaned down and gently pressed his lips to hers. The kiss was over almost before it began. Reluctantly he straightened and unfolded a towel.

"Raise your arms," he commanded wrapping the towel around her with its ends at her back.

"What are you doing?" she asked.

He smiled at her. "Something I'm sure you're going to enjoy. Now lay back and relax."

And enjoy she did.

She lay on the bed with her feet at the bottom edge of the mattress. He moved the pillow down to cushion her head. After pouring the warm oil in the palms of his hands, he pressed, rubbed, and stroked away

the tension in her foot. She closed her eyes, letting
her body luxuriate in the pleasure of his hands and
the soft music. She opened her eyes briefly when she
felt him drape the second towel across her hips and
closed them again as his large hands spread the oil
from her thigh to her ankle, working muscle group
by muscle group until long, pleasurable minutes later
both legs were warmed, oiled, and totally relaxed.

"Anna May, lift up a little," he said sliding his
hands on her back. With very little effort on her part,
he slid the teddy down to her waist, arranging the
towel so that only her breasts were covered and leaving the other towel at her hips. His oil-slick hands
massaged her sides, easing the tense muscles into a
relaxed state. When her shoulders, arms, and hands
were oiled and relaxed, she opened her eyes.

"Thanks, Ric," she said, her voice husky and soft.

"You're welcome, but I'm not done yet," he said
wiping his hands on the ends of her towel. He kneeled
on the mattress, positioning himself in the space
between the headboard and her pillow.

"Sit up for a second." When she did, he moved
forward and kneeled behind her. He tossed her pillow
aside and placed a thin decorative pillow between his
legs. He held out his hand and she lay on her back
with her head on the pillow. "Comfortable?"

"Umm, yes" she replied closing her eyes.

"Good," he said encircling her chin and jaw with
his hands. The warmth of his hands penetrated her
skin like a caress. Then he drew his hands slowly and
gently over her jaw until the tips of his fingers brushed
her ears. He traced the outer edge of her ears, she
trembling at his touch.

"You like that?" he asked, his voice smooth, deep,
and as gentle as his touch.

"Yes, I like it," she said opening her eyes to meet his dark, sensuous gaze.

He repeated the caress. "You have very pretty lips," he said tracing the shape of her mouth with his fingertips. "They're soft"—he stroked her upper lip—"warm,"—he traced her bottom lip then slipped his finger between them. Her heart quickened when he brought his finger to his lips, "And very sweet."

He placed his hands on her shoulders, kneading and caressing. Creating tension and sharp sparks of pleasure with every stroke of his hand. Gone was the relaxed, floating on a cloud feeling he'd invoked.

Anna May watched his face as he molded his hands on her back, gliding upward along the sides of her ribs. When he reached her shoulders, he used the backs of his hands to stroke her from her shoulders to her hands, entwining his fingers with hers; he lifted her arms and gently moved them until her arms outstretched over her head on the mattress.

With his fingertips at her breastbone, he eased his hands between her breasts, dragging the towel down until her chest was bare. He swept his hands over her stomach, then pulled them along her sides, molding his hands around the sides of her breasts, circling around until he cupped her breasts in his hands. Slowly he circled his palms around her breasts. Her heart thundered in her chest as he repeated the caress again and again, deliberately avoiding her nipples until she couldn't stand it any longer.

"Ric?" she said hardly recognizing the thick, throaty voice as her own.

"Yes," he murmured.

"Touch me."

His laugh was short and choppy. "Honey, I am touching you. Can't you feel it?"

She arched her back as he circled her breasts again, the tips of his fingers coming closer to the desired spot. Over and over he caressed her, coming near but never quite touching her where she yearned to be touched. Her lips parted and a single tear slid down her cheek as his hands both gave and denied her pleasure.

He stopped when he saw her tear. "Don't cry," he said, then tenderly brushed his fingertips over the top of her nipples, drawing a harsh cry from her lips.

Heat radiated from her breasts to the center of her body. As he gently touched her body, pleasure like she'd never known settled inside her, growing tighter and stronger with every stroke. She cried out as he teased her nipples, circling the brown orbs before drawing them between his thumb and forefinger. She moaned in frustration when he took away his hands.

"It's okay. I'm not going anywhere." He shifted his weight to his knees, quickly removing his shirt, then moving his body until he lay down beside her. He cupped his hand under her breast then leaned forward. The feel of his mouth on her body sent blasts of heat between her legs. From a distance she heard herself sob, but there was nothing she could do to stop.

"Do you like that, Anna May, or do you like this better?" He scraped his tongue over the tip of her nipple.

She arched her back as desire washed over her.

"Which do you like?"

"Both."

"Both it is," he murmured.

The strange tension in her body magnified with every stroke of his tongue and every suckle he took from her breast. No man had ever touched her like this, giving her this kind of intense pleasure.

"Ric ... Ric ... please."

He eased his hand down her stomach underneath the towel until he reached the lace fabric. Moving his hand between her legs, he rotated his thumb back and forth. She moved her hips, questing and seeking relief from the unbearable tension inside her.

She closed her eyes as spots of bright, intense light danced before her eyes. The tight coil of tension sprang free, sending her free falling into an intense, burning pleasure.

Chapter Eight

Ric watched as Anna May slowly opened her eyes. His need burned like a raging fire, wild, powerful. It had taken nearly everything inside him not to rip off the lacy strips that barely covered her and bury himself inside her when she rocked her hips against his hand and cried out her release.

He hadn't. Not then.

As if she'd read his thoughts, she blushed and reached for the towel to cover herself.

"No," he said softly. "Don't hide your beautiful body from me," he said as he covered her hand with his.

"I . . . I . . ."

He brushed his lips across hers in a soft-as-a-butterfly kiss. "There's nothing to be embarrassed about. Passion is a natural part of life."

"I know, but I didn't expect it."

"You didn't? What did you expect?" he asked as he kissed her flushed cheek.

"I don't know. I know you don't love me. I guess I didn't think I or you would enjoy this," she said, her voice trailing off in embarrassment.

He raised his head and looked into her brown eyes. Did she really think he'd treat making love to her as a job? Something to do quickly and get it over with? Her sincere belief in the statement was unmistakable. Besides, he'd never known her to lie to him. He smiled. He'd have to prove to her just how wrong she was. His smile deepened and darkened with anticipation as he thought of hearing the sound of her release again.

"So you thought you'd have to lie back and think of England? Anna May, we've barely begun to enjoy ourselves." He kissed her lips softly then stood beside the bed. His fingers quickly loosened the belt at his waist, and the soft music muffled the sound of his zipper. He took off his pants, removing his briefs with them.

Her gasp aroused him further. Ahh, yes, he thought as he lay on the bed. He'd definitely make sure she enjoyed every minute of their time together. He gathered her in his arms, her soft breasts pressing against his chest, her hips pressing against his, separated by the silky bit of lace.

"We never did get you out of this," Ric said in a thick tone. "I think it's about time we did." He sat up then slid the lacy creation down her hips and legs.

He let his gaze feast on her lush breasts, slender waist, and full womanly hips.

"I wish I had the words to tell you how beautiful you are," he said hoarsely. He reached out, taking her hand and placing her palm over his heart. "Maybe I can show you instead."

He lay down on his side facing her. Leaning forward, he kissed her soft lips. He felt her put her arm around his shoulder. Her hand trembled as she rubbed his shoulders. He realized that she trembled from nerves, not from passion. Slowly he opened his eyes, studying her tightly closed eyelids and quivering lips.

"Anna May," he whispered.

She opened her eyes.

"Kiss me," he said rolling onto his back.

She looked at him with wariness in her eyes. Finally she leaned down and briefly placed her lips on his.

"Not like that. Like this," he said placing his hand behind her head. He kissed her with all the gentleness he had inside him. Brushing his lips over hers in a soft, lazy motion until her tense shoulders relaxed against him and her soft breasts burned against his chest. Again and again he kissed her until her lips followed his. Until he couldn't tell if he was kissing her or she was kissing him.

"Anna May," he said thickly. Waiting until her hot brown gaze met his he added, "Touch me."

"Where?"

"Anywhere you want, honey. Anywhere."

She moved off his chest and lay on her side beside him. He wanted to tell her to come back, missing the warmth and fire of her body. She touched his face, gliding her finger down his cheek, then softly outlining his mouth. He parted his lips and used his tongue to taste her.

Reaching up, he copied the same path across her cheeks and lips. He groaned in satisfaction when her tongue grazed the tips of his fingers. He traced her chin and jaw, sliding his fingertips down her neck to the base of her throat. Pausing, he felt the rapid beat of her pulse. He leaned forward and kissed her throat.

She trembled and he smiled in the darkness. Lying back on his pillow, he waited and watched her response. He didn't have long to wait. She followed the hard line of his jaw, caressing his neck, and kissed his throat. She kneaded his shoulder as she spread kisses along his collarbone. Down and down her soft lips traveled over the hard ridge of his chest, sending waves of delight down his body. She paused when she reached his nipple. He held his breath as she brushed her slightly parted lips over his nipple. He stiffened and groaned as she suckled him, her strokes were tentative and unsure, nonetheless they aroused him until he was almost beyond control.

He brushed his hand through her hair, gently urging her to still her deliciously arousing mouth. "Stop, Anna May," he said taking ragged gasps of air.

She stopped. Lifting her head, she looked at him. Her cheeks were flushed with passion and her brown eyes burned brightly with desire. "Don't you like it?"

His laugh was rough and harsh. "Yes, honey. I like it a lot." He took her hand and closed it around his manhood. "I like it."

Her gasp was a mixture of wonder and surprise.

When he moved his hand, hers stayed curved around him. His jaw clenched as she hesitantly explored the length and width of him with her soft curious hand.

Ric groaned and his muscles flexed.

"Sorry," she said withdrawing her hand.

"There's nothing to be sorry for," he said returning her hand to his flesh. When he was sure she wouldn't withdraw from him, he caressed her shoulder then rubbed the back of his fingers over her breast before traveling down the smooth, satiny slope of her torso and stomach. He smiled in pleasure as the muscles in her stomach trembled beneath his hand.

He withstood her caress for as long as he could. Taking her hand away from his body, he sat up then lifted and settled her astride his hips, bringing their bodies as close as possible without entering her. Her eyes darkened as he lowered his head.

He kissed her in wild hunger. Slipping his tongue between her lips thrusting and retreating in a dance as old as man. Her groan sent a shudder of desire through him, which intensified as her arms wrapped around him. He ran his fingers through her hair. He ended the kiss with a moan when she rocked her hips in an unconscious invitation. He rocked his hips gently. Her breath broke, and her nails bit faintly on his back.

"Ric," she moaned when he rocked his hips again. With her head back, she moved her hips. The harsh, short breath felt warm against his cheek. He slid his hand down her shoulder. Taking her hand, he guided her to his manhood.

"Take me inside you," he said.

Together they joined their bodies. She was tight, so very hot, he thought as he slowly eased inside her. He found the barrier of her innocence. Swearing inwardly, he pushed against the barrier.

"Oh," she moaned.

Sweat gathered on his brow as he pressed. The barrier held firmly in place. Slowly he met her anxious gaze. With sorrow, he said, "Hold on to me." As her arms tightened around him, he wrapped his hands around her buttocks and rocked firmly against her.

Her nails bit deeply into his skin, and he felt her barrier give way. He remained still inside her, wanting to thrust and move but afraid to cause her more pain. Gently he moved his hands up and down her back.

"I'm sorry, honey," he said stroking her until he felt the tension in her body ease. "Are you all right?"

"I . . . I think so," she whispered.

Leaning back he said, "Look at me."

She leaned back, moving ever so slightly.

He sucked in his breath as her muscles tightened around him. "Are you sore? Does that hurt?" His voice was harsh with desire he held at bay.

She tensed the muscles inside her again. "No. It doesn't hurt anymore."

Closing his eyes in relief, he rocked slowly against her. "Okay?" he asked.

"Okay," she said.

He placed his hands on her hips and moved her forward as he rocked again. "Okay?"

"Yes."

Again and again their hips moved together and apart, building the tension inside him until he thought he would explode. But he didn't want to make the journey without her. He felt the change in her body as they continued to move. Her hands moved almost frantically on his back, her hips moved firmly and purposely over his, and the sweet sound of her delight rang in his ear.

He moved harder searching for the rhythm that would give her the release they so desperately sought. Her hips thrust wildly against his, matching him thrust for thrust. He felt his control slipping away with every move. Fire burned inside him. "Anna May, Anna May," he chanted as his body moved closer to ecstasy. Then her arms tightened around him, and she screamed her release. What little control he had left shattered, and he tumbled over the edge into ecstasy.

* * *

Somehow he'd found the strength to get them both under the covers. He lay on his side, holding Anna May in a spoonlike fashion. Anna May, his friend, his wife, his lover. The passion inside her surprised him. Never in his wildest dreams had he thought she'd want him. He would never forget the feel of her body moving over his or the sound of her passionate scream.

She wanted him.

But only for a little while. Only until she became pregnant with his child. He curved his arm around her waist, letting his hand spread over her flat stomach. Their child could be growing inside her now. Fierce pride and protectiveness flowed in his veins. His child. In the stillness of the night, he admitted to himself that he wanted her child almost as much as he wanted her.

The pale morning sun peeked through the windows in Ric's bedroom. Anna May lay on her side, watching as the weak rays of sunshine lit up the room. She was well and truly married now, she thought. The weight of Ric's arm over her waist felt heavenly, and the feel of his hand resting over her stomach made her shiver.

Last night had been a dream come true for her. She'd made love to Ric. The man she loved. She wasn't going to lie to herself. The love was all on her end. But he'd made her first experience with making love a memorable one. The pleasure, and even the pain, were all stored in the memory of her mind. She knew one day her memories would be all that she had left of tonight. Unless, she'd gotten pregnant. Hope sprang forth. *Forget it Anna May. What are the odds of getting pregnant the first time? Slim to none.* But hope once kindled was hard to hold at bay. Gently she placed her hand over Ric's and closed her eyes, trying to imagine her stomach round with child. Instead, she saw herself holding a sturdy little boy about two years old, a perfect miniature of Ric. She smiled and held on to that image. As she drifted into sleep, she thought she heard the sound of a child calling for his mama.

The sun was shining brightly when she awoke again. The familiar weight of Ric's arm was missing from her waist. Disappointed but slightly relieved, she slowly opened her eyes and looked directly into Ric's warm brown eyes.

"Morning," he said in a husky voice.

Heat rushed to her face, and her heart skipped a beat. "Morning," she whispered averting her gaze and pulling the covers up to her chin.

He put his hand under her chin, raising it until she looked at him. "Don't be shy with me."

"I can't help it, Ric. I've never done this before and it's embarrassing."

"What's embarrassing?"

"Ric! We're naked."

He lifted the cover and looked under it. He pulled the cover over his chest and said in a shocked tone of voice, "Damn. You're right. How'd that happen?"

"Ric," Anna May groaned.

"Anna May, we're alone. Nobody cares if we're naked. Most people expect newlyweds to be naked the day after the wedding."

"I know," she replied. "I guess I'll have to get used to it."

"You plan on being naked a lot?" he asked with a straight face.

She closed her eyes briefly as shyness warred with amusement.

"Who would have thought Pastor Robinson's daughter likes being naked? Hummph, hummph, hummph."

"Stop," she said putting her hands over her warm face.

He smiled at her. "Don't worry. Your secret's safe with me."

"I don't have a secret."

He put his hand over his heart. "You mean everybody knows you like to be naked. Was I the last to know?"

"You rat." She laughed.

His smile faded. "Yeah, but you're not trying to hide under the covers anymore."

"I know it's silly, but I've spent all my life being alone. Now I'm sleeping naked with a man. I've never slept naked in my life. It's going to be a major adjustment for me."

"I know. If it helps, I'll wear pajamas to bed," he said.

"Do you have a pair?"

"No, but for you I'll go and buy a pair."

"Thanks, but that's not necessary," she said. "I'll get used to it. Maybe one day I'll look back on this conversation and laugh."

"Maybe. So how are you feeling? Are you sore?" he asked—gone was the playful tone, replaced with concern.

"No, I feel fine," she said feeling embarrassed by their frank conversation.

"Good. I didn't want to hurt you," he said softly as he touched her cheek.

"You didn't," she murmured shyly, remembering the passion he'd given her.

"Yes, I did at first."

"But you didn't in the end," she replied. "You made me feel so good, so wanted."

"I'm glad," he said softly then cleared his throat. "So you want first dibs on the bathroom?"

She wanted to say yes but to do so would mean walking across the room totally naked. She wasn't ready for that. "No. You go ahead."

"You sure? I promise to keep my eyes closed," he said.

She was really tempted to take him up on the offer. "You promise?" she asked.

"I promise," he replied.

"Okay." She waited until she saw him close his eyes before she slid from under the covers.

When she was in the middle of the room, he said, "Anna May, I didn't say when I'd close my eyes." She glanced over her shoulder. There lying with his hands behind his head, his eyes wide open, was her husband. She turned and ran the rest of the way to the bathroom.

"That was a rotten thing to do, Ric," Anna May said when she walked into the bedroom wearing her robe.

"No more rotten than the time you stole my clothes while I was swimming this summer," he replied.

"How was I supposed to know you were in the buff?

Nobody told you to go skinny dipping in the first place."

"I own the lake. I can do what I want. And what I want right now," he said flipping back the covers, "is a hot shower."

She caught her breath as he walked toward her naked as the day he was born. He had a beautiful body. Strong, hard, and completely male. When he reached her, he kissed her forehead.

"Try not to stare the next time," he said then walked out of the room.

She stared at the closed bathroom door then smiled. For a man who had to be talked into marrying her, he was treating her with the same teasing friendship he'd shown her in the past. Granted the topic of his teasing was more intimate, and at times embarrassing—nonetheless he'd still offered her his friendship.

Anna May smiled and walked to the closet. Things were going to be okay, she thought. She wouldn't lose her best friend after all.

Twenty minutes later Ric entered the kitchen. She smiled as he entered the room. "You want bacon or sausage?" she asked stirring the grits.

"I'll have whatever you're having. Do you want any help?" he asked.

"No, everything's almost done."

This was the first meal they'd shared privately as a married couple, and she wanted to prepare it herself.

"So what do you have planned for today?" she asked as she added more bacon.

"Nothing that couldn't wait if you have something else in mind."

His answer sent ripples of desire through her body.

"I didn't have anything else in mind," she said breathlessly.

"I'm going to Home Depot. I need to pick up a new drill bit."

"What are you working on now?"

"I'm making a room in the attic."

She listened as he explained what he was planning to add in the room. She had no doubt that he'd do exactly what he said he'd do. Carpentry was his hobby and like everything else he did, he did it well.

When she was satisfied with the meal, she set the food on the table. Her grits were smooth, the bacon crisp, the eggs were scrambled just the way he liked them, and the biscuits were golden brown.

"This is good," he said. "I usually don't cook on the weekends."

"I don't know why you don't hire a chef. It would be a lot simpler and easier on you."

"The housekeeper, Mrs. Thompson, is enough. I don't want that many people to have access to my house. This is the one place where I know everything will be like I left it."

"We're only talking about the kitchen and maybe the dining room."

He shook his head. "No, I don't want one."

"Well, we're going to have to talk about the cooking arrangements because I normally cook on the weekends. During the week I'm usually tired. So why don't we work up a schedule to split the cooking duty."

"You don't have to cook if you don't want to. Don't change your habits because of me."

Don't change your habits, she thought. If she had her way, she'd change her whole life. "I think it's only fair that we split the work around here. I don't want you to think I'm freeloading. I want to do my share.''

"How about one person cooks and the other person cleans up?" he replied.

"That seems fair.''

"It's right up my alley because I'd rather cook than clean.''

"You sound like James. He always paid me to do the kitchen when it was his week to take care of the kitchen.'' She smiled as she remembered fun she had with her brothers growing up. "Oh, did I tell you James is moving back to Atlanta?''

"No. Did he get transferred?''

"Yes—his company gave him a three-year assignment. I didn't know financial people were in such great demand.''

"Managers have a tendency to get a little excited when the numbers are published,'' he said.

"I know, but they're paying him big bucks and all he does is run reports and spreadsheets.''

"I think James would disagree with you. Financial officers aren't paid the kind of money they are by running reports that any clerical person could run.''

"I know, but it irritates him every time I say it. I've got to get my licks in early with him.''

"Why do you fight with him? You and Steven seem to get along fine, but if James said something's black, you'd argue that it was white.''

"I think James and I are too much alike, and it's entirely too much fun to see who'll win the argument,'' she said with a smile.

He laughed. "All these years, I thought you just liked to argue with me.''

"I do like arguing with you. You're Mr. Cool-Calm-and-Collected businessman most of the time, and people fawn over you. I like to ruffle your image because you need it every once in a while."

"I need it?"

"Yes. You're so serious, and at times you'll tend to forget to laugh. I'm just a friendly reminder that life can be so funny," she said.

"So you think I'm too serious?" he asked.

"I know you are."

He frowned and continued to eat his meal in a comfortable silence. Anna May waited for his response, and when none was forthcoming, she finished her meal. From years of experience, she knew he was thinking on what she said to him. She liked knowing that he listened to her. He might not agree with what she said, but he listened. She felt as if she could tell him anything. Well, almost anything.

She couldn't tell him she loved him and wanted their marriage to last "until death do us part." Her only hope was for Ric to fall as deeply in love with her as she was with him. If only she knew how to make him love her.

Home Depot was crowded with Sunday afternoon shoppers. Stacked with tools and building supplies, it was a do-it-yourselfer's paradise. She smiled as they walked through the huge warehouse and wondered what her friends would think if they saw her. Honeymoon in Home Depot didn't have a romantic ring to it, but she was enjoying herself because she was with her husband.

In tan corduroy pants and navy wool sweater, Ric was slightly overdressed in a crowd wearing jeans and sweatshirts. Even overdressed, he had a commanding air about him.

"So what did we come here for?" she asked following him down an aisle filled with plumbing material.

"A drill bit."

"What does it look like?"

"Like a drill bit."

"Ha, ha, ha," she said. "Do you know where you're going?"

"Yes, I'm in here a lot." He led her to the corner of the store where row after row of power tools were on display. An older man wearing a bright orange apron with the name "Grady" written in black letters approached them. His short Afro was so totally gray that it seemed almost white against his dark brown skin.

"Good morning, Mr. Justice. What can I do for you today?" the man asked.

Anna May raised her brow. He was in this store more than she realized if the employees knew him by name.

"Good morning. I'm looking for a drill bit."

She stood to the side as they talked about bit diameters and working surfaces of which her knowledge of either was null.

He looked so handsome standing there, leaning forward as if listening intently to the shorter man. An aura of power and strength surrounded him, even in the relaxed atmosphere of the store.

Her body tingled as she remembered the strength and power he'd used last night. She was eager to feel his power again soon.

Ric nodded, keeping one of the two packages in his hand and returning the other to the shelf.

"Are you ready?" Ric asked.

She nodded in response.

"Anna May, this is Grady. Grady, this is my wife, Anna May Justice."

Grady's gray eyebrows lifted in surprise. "Congratulations," he said while shaking her hand. "I wish you both the best."

"Thank you," she said.

As they walked to the front of the store, she said, "He seemed like a nice man."

Ric shrugged. "He knows power tools."

Suddenly a little boy ran up to them.

"Come here, John." A younger man wearing faded jeans rushed forward. The toddler looked at the man then looked at Ric and ran to Ric, grabbing Ric's pant leg when he stopped. The man was joined by a woman carrying a purse and a diaper bag. The man scooped up the little boy and held him in his arms.

"Sorry about that. He got away from me for a second," he said.

"That's okay," Ric replied.

The man put his arm around the woman's shoulders and walked away. Anna May felt a longing in her heart. She wanted what the couple had. She wanted a family of her own.

Chapter Nine

She was a long way from happily ever after, Anna May thought as she listened to the sound of a hammer pounding against wood on the floor above her. When they'd returned from Home Depot, she didn't think twice when he'd told her he was going to work on the attic for a little while. She thought it was a good idea at the time. Her suitcases were full of clothes that needed to be unpacked.

Now two hours later all of her clothes were put away, and she had nothing but time on her hands. She fluffed a pillow on the already immaculate bed. It had taken her a few minutes to straighten the bedroom. If she was at her other home, she would have found things to do to keep herself occupied, but this was her home only temporarily, and she was reluctant to change things without his permission.

To be honest, she didn't really want to do anything but be with her husband, and from the amount of noise he was making, it would be a while before he finished.

Ric mindlessly pounded the nails into the drywall. It was that or go downstairs and make love to his wife. His body hardened as he remembered her innocent caresses and the startled cries of passion.

Last night was a night he would never forget. So why was he upstairs in the attic and his wife was somewhere downstairs? he wondered. He'd convinced himself that he was giving her time. Time to become accustomed to an intimate relationship. But he knew he wasn't being truthful. He was hiding, keeping himself at a distance because it wouldn't be hard for him to fall in love with her.

"Love," he muttered in disgust as he pounded the hammer into another nail. He didn't trust love. To him the word had no real meaning. His mother had told him over and over again that she loved him, yet she'd let other people raise him while she and his little brother lived a life of luxury. If that was love, then he didn't need it.

What he was feeling for Anna May was lust, he told himself. Pure animal attraction—and it would soon die down as they became more familiar with each other. Familiar with her smooth brown skin, familiar with the sweet jasmine scent at her breasts, familiar with her soft, silky thighs. Cursing, he stepped away from the wall. Putting up drywall wasn't having the calming effect he'd expected. He was just as aroused now as he was when he watched the sway of her hips in Home Depot.

A pencil-thin model she was not. Her blue jeans hugged her full, curvy hips and small waist. She had the kind of lush curves that made him think of all the wicked, naughty things he'd like to do with her.

As much as he wanted her, and regardless of the fact that they were married, he knew his time with her was temporary. She wanted a child, and he was just the means to give her one. He'd be doing them both a favor if he remembered that.

Determined, he focused his attention on the wall in front of him. He would have to build a wall as thick as the one he was putting up to keep his feelings at bay. With a swing of the hammer, another nail anchored the drywall. He only wished guarding his heart was as easy.

"Don't you want to open the gifts?" Anna May asked from the doorway with her arms folded across her chest.

Ric smiled to himself behind the Sunday paper. She was like a kid in a candy store, and she couldn't wait to open the wedding gifts they'd received. Her hints had gone from subtle to downright blatant in the hour since he'd finished working in the attic. Crossing his legs at the ankle, he lowered the newspaper and pretended to consider her question.

"No, we can open them later," he said in a casual, disinterested tone.

"When?" she demanded.

He shrugged his shoulders and began reading the paper again. "Maybe tomorrow when I come home from work."

"Riiiccc," she cried.

"What?"

"I can't wait that long. I want to open them now."

"Go ahead," he answered as he turned the page of the newspaper.

"You don't want to open them with me?"

He almost laughed at her incredulous tone. "No, you go ahead. I'll finish reading the paper."

Anna May walked over to his chair and snatched the paper out of his hands. "You can finish the paper later. Let's open the presents now," she said, then added a moment later when he hadn't moved from his chair, "please."

He looked at the newspaper in her hand with exaggerated longing. "All right," he said then smiled mischievously. "But I get to open the first one."

Smiling she dropped the paper on the floor, then took his hand and pulled him from his seat. "I don't care. Let's go."

The living room was masculine, cold, and elegant. The interior decorator Ric had hired when he bought the house had designed the room with power and money in mind. It was not, Anna May thought, meant to be used except on certain important business occasions. She had been in this room twice, once when Ric gave her a tour of the house and now.

The antique oak table in the living room was piled with richly wrapped gifts which the chauffeur had brought inside for them last night.

"Which one do you want to open first?" she asked as she pulled him inside the room.

Looking over the assorted gifts, he chose the smallest one. Side by side they sat on the sofa. He took his time opening the gift, careful not to tear the gold foil wrapping paper.

"Hurry, Ric," she said with a little impatience and a lot of excitement.

"If I hurry, I'll rip the paper," he responded.

"So rip the paper."

"But then the gift won't last as long," he said.

"What?"

"When I was little, I thought my gift would last longer if I took my time unwrapping it." He laughed self-consciously. "Funny, the things you remember from your childhood," he said peeling off the tape.

"My gifts would have lasted all of five seconds—I'm a ripper when it comes to presents. On Christmas or my birthday, I could hardly wait to take off the paper and see what was inside. Sometimes I'd even help my brothers open their gifts. *That* didn't go over too well sometimes. I didn't care if the gift cost two dollars or two hundred dollars, I just thought it was exciting to find out what was inside."

His laugh was harsh and mocking. "When I stayed with my grandmother, I always knew what was inside the box. Every year at Christmas I got a recycled toy from the church charity, and on my birthday the same charity gave me a set of new clothes."

She placed her hand on his hard thigh. "Oh, your grandmother couldn't afford to get toys for you?"

"She could afford it all right. She didn't want to waste the money my mother gave her on me."

"Your mother sent her money? I don't understand. Why weren't you living with your mother?" Anna May knew why he wasn't living with his mother. Ric's aunt and uncle had told her about his past, but this was the first time Ric had spoken about it, and she wanted to hear it from him.

"She remarried, and my stepfather didn't want me around especially when my mother had his son."

"What's your brother's name, and why haven't you told me about him?"

He frowned. "There was no reason for you to hear

about him. His name is Adam Wilson. For all I know, he doesn't know I exist.''

"I've known you for almost twenty years, and you've never said anything about your brother and barely mentioned your mother. What else haven't you told me? What else don't I know about you?''

"You know me," he said pointing to his heart. "You know what I like and you know what I don't like. You're the only person in the world who knows the real me, not the businessman, not the Ice Man, but plain old Ric Justice. So you didn't know about my brother, and I don't talk about my mother. So what? I know my brother and my mother didn't make me the person I am today.''

"But you are her family. How could she treat you like that?'' she said hotly. She didn't want to think ill of the dead, but what she was learning about his mother made her blood boil.

"Easy,'' he said casually as he removed the last piece of tape. Noting the department store logo on the box, he removed the top. He froze and stared at the contents inside the box.

"What it is?'' she asked and glanced inside. Matching sterling silver picture frames were nestled inside, behind the glass were old pictures. One was of a man dressed in a military uniform holding a baby. The other was a picture made at the time same, with the man holding the baby in one arm and his other arm around the shoulders of a young woman. Anna May recognized the features of Ric's aunt. As she looked closer, she noticed similar features in the man.

"Who's that with your aunt?'' she asked.

"My father and I,'' he said picking up a frame.

"What a nice gift. Do you have many pictures of your father?''

"No. I have one other picture of him that Aunt Betty gave to me when I moved in with them," he replied as he gave her the box.

Anna May picked up one of the frames, but her attention wasn't on the gift. For as long as she'd known Ric, he'd never really talked about his life before he moved in with his aunt and uncle. He'd kept himself distant from them, although he'd lived with them for four years. Ric had never known what it was like to have a real family. He had a family with an aunt and uncle he kept at arm's length, a little brother he hadn't seen in years, and a wife who loved him. Placing the frame inside the box, she vowed to show him a different type of family. Starting with herself, her family, and later his family, she planned to show him a real family.

A loving family.

"I'd better get a box of thank-you cards tomorrow," she said with her thoughts filled with plans to reunite him and his relatives.

"Hmm."

"Don't worry, I'll do the cards since I'm not going to go to work tomorrow."

"Oh. What do you plan to do all day?"

"I'm going to unpack some of my things. Put up pictures of my family, set up my computer. Things like that. You know—adding little things here and there around the house. But I won't change anything major."

"This is your house, too. Change anything you want."

"I don't think you want me to do that," she said looking around the starkly traditional living room. "We have totally different styles, and I don't want you to think that I'm trying to take over your house."

"You've got to be comfortable here. I don't want you to feel like a guest. For as long as we're married, this is *our* house. Not yours. Not mine, but ours."

For as long as we're married, Anna May mused to herself. They were going to stay married for as long as they lived if she had anything to do with it. She wanted to be such an integral part of his life that he wouldn't think of divorcing her.

She smiled shyly at him. "You'll tell me if you don't like something I've done, won't you?"

He raised his brows. "When have you ever known me *not* to tell you I don't like something?"

"Never."

"I'm glad we've got that settled. Now are you going to open a gift, or should I go finish reading the paper?"

She picked up the biggest box on the table, then tore the wrapping paper. "No way. We're opening all the gifts tonight."

Ric leaned back against the sofa. "If you're opening the rest of them, it will only take two minutes."

It took her ten minutes to open the remaining packages. Bright pieces of wrapping paper clashed with the staid yet elegant wool rug.

"Is that the last one?" he asked, referring to the Waterford crystal vase.

"That's it," she said, carefully placing the vase in the box. "This vase would look good on the table over there with fresh-cut flowers to add a touch of color to the room. There's no color in this room," she stated, crinkling her nose.

"There is color in the room. Black, white, and gray are colors."

"Yeah, but they're dull colors. You need a touch

of red in here. This room makes me feel like I'm in a black-and-white photograph."

"What do you want to do to change it? Other than the flowers?" he asked.

"Not a lot. I'd add a few pillows, a few knickknacks just to make the room a little friendlier."

He turned, giving her a puzzled look. "Make the room friendlier?"

"This is a very unfriendly room. It doesn't give you the feeling that you're welcome to linger and chat. It's cool and intimidating. It's not like you at all."

"Really. What am I like?" he asked crossing his arms across his chest, his brown eyes dark with curiosity.

She pursed her lips, leaning her head to the side. "You are the nicest man I've ever met. Although you do try to hide it from people. You're real. You accept people the way they are." She shrugged her shoulders. "I don't know . . . you're not the stereotypical CEO type. I couldn't talk to anyone else the way I talk to you, not even my family."

"I don't think my competitors think of me as nice."

"They don't know you. I know you. I don't think another man would have agreed to help me the way you have. You've done everything to make me comfortable from the beginning." She took his hand in hers. "Thank you. I couldn't have asked for a better friend than you."

"You make me sound like a saint. I'm definitely no saint."

"I know that, and I'm not saying that you're a saint but you're a whole lot nicer than you pretend to be."

"Nice," he said softly. "A man doesn't want to be known as nice. That's such a bland description of a person. It brings to mind the saying, 'Nice guys finish last.' "

She shook her head and said, "I don't think you'll ever be last in anything unless you want to be."

He raised his eyebrows in surprise, then drew them together in a frown. "You have a lot of faith in my abilities. Don't be disappointed if I don't live up to your standards."

"You won't disappoint me," she said with certainty as she studied his troubled face. "You never have." When his frown deepened, she turned her attention to the room again. "Red. This room definitely needs a splash of red."

She continued a steady dialog of decorating ideas until the line between his brow faded and the tense muscles in his jaw relaxed.

You won't disappoint me.

Anna May's words replayed in his mind as he lay naked on top of the wrinkled bedsheets. The musky smell of sex from their recent lovemaking filled the dimly lit bedroom, and her warm body snuggled next to his in sleep.

She had no idea how her words affected him, he thought, as he stared into the darkness. Her unfailing faith in him never ceased to surprise him. It wasn't as if he tried to hide the bad side of himself, it just seemed that she was never around when he was at his worst. Sooner or later it was going to happen, and he wondered how she would react?

He lay still as she moved closer to him, her leg rested on top of his, her soft bare breast pressed against his chest, and her head lay on his shoulder. When she settled back into sleep, he put his arm around her shoulder. Contentment filled him as he touched her satiny skin.

She'd been living in his house for only a day, and he could already see it would be so easy for him to get used to having her in his house, in his bed. She would leave him and he knew it, like his mother had left him. As a boy he had been at the mercy of his mother's whims. As a man he was at the mercy of no one, not even his innocent, sexy, and temporary wife.

When this marriage came to an end, he planned to keep his heart untouched and unscathed as he had in his past relationships.

The women in his past hadn't satisfied him as his wife had tonight with her own brand of innocent seduction.

The women in his past hadn't been his best friends.

The women in his past weren't Anna May.

As his eyelids grew heavy with sleep and the defenses he used to guard his heart relaxed, he wondered how he would resist falling in love with her. Just before he fell asleep, he admitted to himself that he couldn't.

Anna May stretched, drawing her body slowly and lazily against her husband's still form. She looked up at her husband's relaxed face. Even in his sleep, Ric looked hard and in control. His jaw, though relaxed, was firm and his long black lashes rested against his strong cheeks.

She longed to touch his face but she hesitated, unsure of how he would react. Would he welcome her touch, or would he turn away? Although he seemed to enjoy making love with her, she wasn't sure if he would welcome her affection that wasn't a prelude to making love.

Slowly she raised her hand and caressed his cheek with soft, butterfly light strokes. The contrast of the rough stubble of his beard and the warmth of his skin made touching him all the more pleasurable. She followed the downward slope of his cheek, then along the faint laugh line to the edge of his full lips. With the pad of her finger, she leisurely outlined his mouth and tested the firmness of his lips.

He had done so many wicked things with his lips last night, the memory of which made her hand tremble. She'd never known how arousing a single kiss could be until Ric had shown her that her mouth and cheeks weren't the only spots made for kissing. When the tip of her finger returned to the edge of his lips, she let her touch linger, savoring the delightful sensation of her skin against his.

The pattern of his breathing changed, and she raised her head. His gaze was dark, sensuous, and potent. He took her hand, which was still upon his lips, and brushed her fingertips across his firm mouth, once then twice. On the third stroke, he kissed her fingers and held her gaze as he guided her hand to her lips.

"Morning, Anna May," he said. His voice was deep and low.

She kissed her fingers and brought them back to his lips. "Good morning," she whispered.

"It could be," he smiled at her tenderly, wrapping his arm around her waist, pulling her flush to his blatantly aroused body.

"Oh," she said, her eyes widening then darkening as he gently caressed her bare hips.

"Is that an oh yes or an oh no?" His quiet yet deep voice was as much a caress as his hands.

She leaned down and kissed his chest—his skin felt warm against her lips as she made her way to his dark brown nipple, tasting him with the tip of her tongue. Raising her head at the sound of his low, husky moan, she looked at him. His eyelids were lowered, nearly closed, yet his desire for her was clearly visible in his brown eyes.

"That's a definite yes," she whispered.

Chapter Ten

Ric was two hours late for work. As owner of the company, he was usually the first person to arrive and the last to leave. This morning, however, he had been sorely tempted to stay in the bed with the sleeping Anna May. He forced aside the picture in his mind of his wife lying on her stomach, the edge of the sheet draped loosely across her hips.

Glancing at his watch, he quickened his stride as he walked down the hallway to his office. He'd had his secretary reschedule his early morning appointments—however, this meeting had been called months ago, and he couldn't miss it.

"Good morning, Mrs. Jones," he said coming to a stop in front of her desk. "Has Dickerson arrived yet?"

She looked at the clock on her desk. "Good afternoon, Mr. Justice. Mr. Dickerson and Warren are in the conference room now," she said gesturing toward the closed door of the conference room.

Giving her a curt nod, he walked to the door.

J.V. Dickerson was the tallest of the five men in the room. A shade under seven foot, the elderly Texan wore his signature Stetson to perpetuate his image of being a larger-than-life businessman.

Ric remembered a time when the sight of that Stetson had his stomach tied into knots. He had eaten several rolls of antacids before he made his first big sale to the Texas millionaire. With the money Dickerson had paid him for the small drug company, Ric bought two other companies which he turned around financially and sold for a nice big profit. "Justice," Dickerson said in a booming voice, which was in opposition to his age. "How the hell are ya?"

Ric walked across and shook his hand. "I'm fine. Sorry to keep you waiting."

His bright smile smoothed away the wrinkles in his coppery brown skin. "No problem, son. Warren was just filling me in on your recent marriage. If I'd known you were getting married, I'd have postponed the meeting until after your honeymoon." He raised his gray brows and tilted his head to the side. "There's nothing like a honeymoon to really relax a man."

Ric smiled mockingly at the older man. "Relaxation is the last thing I need when I'm doing business with you, Dickerson."

"Yeah, but it sure would have made my job a whole lot easier if it were." He pushed his hat to the back of his head.

"You don't like things easy. It would take all the fun out of trying to convince me to your way of thinking," Ric replied making his way to the conference table.

"My way of thinking is obviously the best. Just ask me and I'll tell you," the older man replied while following Ric to the table where the other three men were sitting.

"I'm sure you will tell me several times during this meeting without my asking. Especially when we start talking about my asking price for Price-Gantt, Inc."

The Texan leisurely sat down in a chair. Stretching his long legs out in front of him, he crossed his ankles. "We need to talk about that, son. I think you're asking for too much money for that company."

Ric gestured for the other men to have a seat before he sat down in the chair next to Dickerson and replied, "And I think I'm asking a fair price."

They negotiated back and forth for the next six hours, stopping only for short breaks to make a few telephone calls, eat lunch while working, and receive faxes. At the end of the day Ric was satisfied with the deal they'd struck.

"Ric, it's always nice to do business with you." Dickerson held out his hand.

"Same here," Ric said as he shook the older man's hand.

"Now that the business is taken care of, my wife would have my hide if I don't invite you and your wife to have dinner with us tonight. She'd get a kick out of meeting the woman that got you to the altar."

Ric nodded his head. "We'd be happy to join you and your wife for dinner."

"You what?" Anna May screeched into the telephone.

Wincing, Ric returned the telephone to his ear. "I accepted an invitation for us to have dinner with my client tonight."

"Ric, can't we postpone dinner until tomorrow? I'll be prepared," she said.

"They'll be leaving town tomorrow morning. Dickerson just bought one of my companies for five and half million dollars. I think we need to have dinner with him."

Holding the phone to her ear, she looked down at the dirty cotton shirt and dusty blue jeans she was wearing. "How long do I have to get ready?"

"They made reservations at Antonio's at eight."

Glancing at the clock on the nightstand, she plopped down on the bed. She had two hours to change, dress, and fight the traffic downtown. "Why didn't you call me sooner?"

Her tone reminded him of the same accusing tone his grandmother used many years ago. "I didn't know he was going to invite us to dinner, and we just got out of the meeting five minutes ago."

She sighed in frustration. "Where do you want me to meet you, at your office?"

"My office is fine."

"All right, I'll get there as soon as I can."

As she had expected, the traffic on the expressway was awful, and when she reached the city, traffic was even worse. A big-name singer was performing at the Fox Theater and cars clogged the streets near Ric's office. As she inched down Peachtree Street, she felt the tension inside her increase. This was her first social function as Mrs. Garrick Justice, and she didn't want to do anything to embarrass herself or him. His short notice didn't help matters, but after she'd calmed down, she realized that he was just as surprised as she was to get the invitation.

Anna May walked into the lobby of Ric's office two hours and fifteen minutes after his call. Cool gray and rose marble lined the wall behind the security guard, and dark winter night seeped inside the remaining glass walls, creating an air of opulence and space.

"Hello. Could you call Mr. Justice, please," she said to the security guard and waited quietly as the young man used the telephone. Studying her reflection in the highly polished glass wall beside her, she brushed her finger through her wind-tossed hair to smooth it back in place. When she was satisfied that her hair was in place, she took a deep breath and forced herself to relax. There was no reason for her to be nervous, she told herself. This was no different than any of the numerous business dinners she'd attended this year. But it was different. She'd always been the business professional, never the spouse. Could she shift roles?

"Miss, he'll be down in a second," the guard said interrupting her thoughts.

She unbuttoned her creme wool coat, melting the chill of winter as waves of warm air flowed in the lobby. The monotone ring of the elevator bell sounded, and she turned as the bright chrome doors slid open.

Ric entered the lobby with his coat folded over one arm and carrying a briefcase in his opposite hand. His charcoal gray suit jacket clung to his broad shoulders. Shoulders she'd clung to this morning as he'd taken her to paradise. Slowly heat reddened her cheeks as she remembered the sweet touch of his hands on her body.

"Are you ready?" he asked when he reached her side.

"Yes."

"The Dickersons will meet us at Antonio's," he said placing the briefcase on the floor.

"Tell me about your client," she said as he put on his coat, then straightened his collar when he'd buttoned it.

He stood motionless while she fussed with his collar. She looked up when she noticed how still he was. The dark heat in his eyes made her stomach tighten. Her mouth felt dry, and she swallowed to clear the sudden lump in her throat. Quickly she moved her hands from his collar and folded them in front of her.

"I've been doing business with J.V. Dickerson since I started this company. He was the first big businessman who saw value in one of the companies I'd bought in Texas. He bought the company from me, but more importantly with his purchase, he made other business owners take a second look at my work." He reached down to pick up his briefcase.

Anna May felt the tension return to her body and with the tension, her uncertainty. This dinner was more important to him than she'd realized. Although he hadn't said it, she was sure Ric wasn't looking forward to dinner with his clients. Was it because she was now involved with this part of his life? Did he resent her intrusion? She'd have to make sure that this dinner went smoothly. Come hell or high water, she thought.

"Are you ready?" he asked.

Lifting her chin, she met his questioning glance then said, "Yes."

They took Ric's Jaguar to Antonio's. On the drive over, Ric told her more about the Texas millionaire. The more he spoke, the more nervous she became. Her imagination went into overdrive as she thought of all the possible things that could go wrong tonight.

Her stomach was in knots when they turned into the parking lot of the restaurant.

Nestled in the heart of Buckhead, Antonio's resembled an antebellum house. Large white columns graced a roomy wraparound porch. Ric gave the valet his keys, then walked to the passenger side and helped her out of the car. They entered what was at one time the foyer. Antique rose wallpaper covered the walls. A tuxedo-clad gentleman smiled when they approached the podium.

"May I help you?" he asked.

"We're with the Dickerson party," Ric replied.

The man looked down for a second. "Yes, the other members have been seated already. Would you like to check your coats?"

Ric raised his eyebrows in question. At her nod, he helped her out of her coat and gave it to the gentleman before removing his own.

"Where's the ladies' room?" she asked the man.

"It's right down the hall, ma'am."

"I'll be just a second," she said to Ric. Her legs felt rubbery as she walked down the hall to the ladies' room. She washed her hands, checked her makeup, and gave herself a mental pep talk before leaving the room.

"I'm ready," she said.

They followed the gentleman down the hall to one of the rooms. Small tables covered with white linen and elegant china dotted the room. Anna May pasted a smile on her face when they were led to a table occupied by an older couple. Her smile slipped briefly when the man rose. Up and up she looked at the man wearing a mocha brown Stetson nearly the same color as his skin and a black suit.

Ric placed his hand at the small of her back. "Anna

May, I'd like you to meet J.V. and Betsy Dickerson. Mr. and Mrs. Dickerson, meet my wife, Anna May Justice.''

"Nice to meet you, Mrs. Justice," the man replied in a voice that matched his height.

"Please call me Anna May," she said then sat in the chair Ric was holding for her.

"Call me J.V.," he replied with a smile.

"Nice to meet you, young lady. I'm Betsy," the older woman said. She was as petite as her husband was tall, as soft spoken as he was loud. They were an interesting couple, Anna May thought.

"J.V. tells me you're newlyweds. How long have you been married?" Betsy asked.

"Three days," Anna May replied.

Betsy gasped in surprise, then turned to her husband. "You didn't tell me they'd only been married three days," she said giving him a hard look.

"You didn't ask," J.V. replied with a frown.

Betsy returned her husband's frown with one of her own before turning to Anna May. "I apologize for interrupting your honeymoon.''

"No need to apologize," Ric replied with a smile.

Betsy looked at Ric then J.V. and shook her head. "I remember my own honeymoon, and I don't think I'd have appreciated having it interrupted by two old geezers.'' Turning her attention to Anna May, she said. "I apologize again for the interruption.''

"Thank you, Betsy," she said.

"Now where's our waiter? I don't know about you, but I'm starving," she said with a smile.

After their waiter had taken their orders, Betsy asked, "So how did you meet?''

"We met when we were in high school," Ric said.

"Oh, were you high school sweethearts?''

"Oh, no," Anna May said. "We were best friends. Besides Ric had all the girls after him in high school."

"Sounds like my J.V. He always had girls running after him," she said giving her husband a teasing look.

"But I knew as soon as I met Betsy, she was the one for me." J.V. took his wife's hand in his own and squeezed it. His love for her was plain to see.

Anna May looked away from the older couple, her heart filled with longing. She wanted Ric to look at her like that . . . with love. Maybe he would one day.

"How long have you been married?" Anna May asked.

"It will be forty-two years this June," Betsy answered.

"Congratulations. That's quite an accomplishment," Anna May said.

"Not really, young lady," J.V. said. "Betsy and I decided we were going to stay married no matter what and that's what we did. That's not an accomplishment, that's sheer stubbornness. Sometimes stubbornness is what keeps your marriage from falling apart."

"We told all five of our children to be ready to give marriage their all because in today's world, marriage is so easily torn apart if both people aren't totally and completely committed to the union." Betsy squeezed J.V.'s hand.

Anna May breathed a sigh of relief when the waiter served the appetizers. She felt as if the words "fraud," "fake," and "phony" were plastered on her chest like a scarlet letter. In the face of the Dickersons' loving marriage, her marriage seemed like quartz compared to the Hope diamond.

As the evening wore on, Anna May felt her deception bearing down on her like a physical weight. The couple spoke freely about their children and were very proud of their eight grandchildren. Betsy showed them a photograph of their youngest grandchild. "This is Jasmine," she said beaming with pride.

"She's adorable," Anna May replied as she looked at the picture of the infant dressed in a pink ruffled dress with a matching hair bow. "She looks like you."

"Do you think so?" she asked, her smile deepening.

Ric leaned over to look at the photograph. He studied the picture then looked at Betsy and said, "She definitely looks like you."

"Are you planning on having a family?" she asked.

"Give them time, Betsy. They just got married," J.V. said.

"We plan on having a child soon," Ric said then turned to her and smiled. Anna May felt her heart race at the sight of his tender expression. He's just trying to impress his clients, she told herself. It isn't real. But her heart refused to listen to her head, and the love she'd tried so hard to contain bubbled to the surface.

"I think it's time for us to leave, Betsy," J.V. laughed.

Ric smiled and said, "I think you're right, J.V. It's time for us to leave."

Evan Wilson watched the two couples from across the dining room. His dinner lay untouched on his plate. Anger and rage had destroyed his appetite. Ric Justice was the cause. He looked so much like his father that he thought he was seeing a ghost when he was escorted to his table, but the man at the table was flesh and blood. The seed of his enemy.

Trevor Justice had been smarter and more handsome than him while growing up, and he'd hated him for it. The Wilson family had money to buy the best. As a teenager, Evan thought he could buy his way above the Justice reputation, but his plan had backfired, and he became known as the snobby rich boy.

But he'd gotten his revenge of sorts. When Trevor died in Vietnam, he married his wife, the woman who'd chosen Trevor over him years ago and made her sorry she'd ever married his enemy. He'd sent Trevor's son to live with his crazy grandmother. If he could have gotten away with it, he would have sent the boy to a workhouse when the old woman died, but Trevor's family had taken the boy in.

The boy was now a man. A very powerful man who could take away his company without blinking.

"Sir? Was the food not to your liking? I can take this back and get you something else if you prefer? Was there something else you'd like?" the waiter said when he looked at Evan's full plate.

What he'd like, Evan thought to himself, is to get rid of Ric Justice. Instead he told the waiter to bring him the menu and he'd choose another entree.

Adam had him banned from entering his own company. Adam was in for a surprise if he thought he could keep him out. There were several men and women at the company who owed him favors. He'd call in a favor, and soon he'd be back in business. What his son didn't realize was people were afraid to lose their jobs, and all he had to do was hint that he could save their jobs and they'd be putty in his hands.

His son had a lot to learn, he thought with a frown. Just because he'd been paid didn't mean he was totally abandoning the company. He still had a few good years left in him, and with his leadership and his son's energy, they could make Wilson and Wilson a strong company again.

He watched as the young woman at his side looked at Justice. She loved him. It was plain to see. Anger boiled inside him. He couldn't let Justice win. It would be like his father winning again.

Somehow, someway he'd find a way to stop Ric Justice. Studying the woman, Evan began to smile as an idea came to mind. Maybe the way to stop Justice was sitting next to him. Evan made a note to find out who the woman was and how he could use her to destroy the man.

"Thank you for coming tonight," Ric said when they'd arrived home. They'd driven to his office to pick up her car, and he'd followed her on the drive home. He dreaded the confrontation with Anna May. She'd been quiet on the short drive to his office, but he was sure that wouldn't be the case when they got home.

"What?" she asked.

"Thank you for having dinner with the Dickersons. We didn't talk about this before we got married. I'll try not to get you involved with my business plans again," he said as they hung their coats in the closet.

She looked at him in surprise. "I didn't have a problem going to dinner with your client. It was the short notice I had a problem with. I know I'll have to attend business and social functions with you just as you'll have to attend some of my business functions. We're no longer single individuals, we're a couple." She closed the closet door and started up the stairs.

"A couple," he said softly as he followed her, surprised and relieved that she wasn't still angry. He'd spent the ride home worrying for nothing. She wasn't mad with him. "A couple," he said again. They were a couple, he thought. He supposed in time he would get used to the idea, even if it was only temporary.

"A couple. You know—like Fred and Ethel, Claire and Cliff. Ric 'n Anna May."

"Ward and June," he added.

"Yeah, but I'm not cleaning house wearing a dress and a strand of pearls." Pausing at the door to the bedroom, she added, "Tell me what you think of the room."

Ric walked in the bedroom. It was the same yet not the same. The sweet smell of flowers greeted him when he entered the room. Large white candles left over from last night were grouped on one of the nightstands beside the bed. A vase full of fresh flowers and Anna May's favorite crystal clock sat on the other. Little items which if looked at separately wouldn't have made a difference, but on the whole made the room seem more welcoming. More like a home where people lived than a very fancy place to sleep.

"Do you like it?" she asked.

Ric turned to her. "I like it."

"Good," she said with a smile.

Her smiled faltered when he loosened the knot of his tie and slid it off. "So what did you think of the Dickersons?" he said turning his back to hide his smile.

"They seem like nice people," she said inching her way to the walk-in closet.

He removed his suit jacket and joined her at the closet door, blocking her means of escape. His heart turned at the sight of her soft, feminine dresses hanging neatly next to his wool-blend suits. Deliberately brushing against her, he reached for a hanger. "I don't think of J.V. as nice. I've had too many business dealings with him to consider him nice. Fair but not nice."

Slipping her shoes off her feet, she placed them on the floor along with her other shoes, which were in a neat line. "I guess my view of him is different because I saw him as a family man."

"I never thought of him as a family man," he said placing the jacket on the hanger. "He always seemed in control to me."

"What does control have to do with family?"

"You lose control when you have a family. Your life is not your own," he said.

"When were you not in control tonight?" She tilted her head to the side and studied him.

Ric frowned. She'd neatly trapped him with his own words. At no time tonight had he felt out of control, and she was his wife. His family.

"I wasn't," he said grudgingly.

"That's what I like about you, Ric. You always admit when you're wrong." She smiled at him and patted his cheek.

"It's only fair. Especially since this is the first time I've ever made a mistake."

She rolled her eyes. "Right. Let me out of here. There's not enough room for the three of us. You, me, and your ego." She placed her hand on his chest as if to push him away.

He wrapped his arms around her waist and pulled her into his embrace. "Is there enough room for you and me?"

Her expression softened at his words. "Maybe," she said shyly.

"I am right about one thing," he said.

"What?"

"I have a very beautiful wife."

"Oh, yeah?" she said as she laid her head on his shoulders.

"Yeah."

"You know what else?" he asked.

"What?"

"We need to get you out of that dress. Now."

Anna May stepped out of his embrace and slowly slid the zipper of her dress down its track.

The temperature in the closet seemed to have elevated by the time she stepped out of her dress. Ric swallowed the lump in his throat at the sight of her partially clad body. The black strapless bra made her breasts seem fuller. He watched in anticipation as she breathed in and out, sure that the slips of satin couldn't contain their bounty. The matching black panties shielded her femininity from view, but it was the thigh-high sheer black stockings that nearly sent him over the edge.

Ric reached out, touching her shoulders, then slid his hand down her arm to take her hand. Raising their joined hands, he kissed her wrist just below her palm. The rapid tempo of her pulse pounded beneath his lips and the seductive smell of perfume enveloped him like a sweet caress. Slowly he placed kiss after soft kiss up her arm to her elbow before placing her hand on his shoulder.

His chest grew tight when he saw her face. Her cheeks were flushed with passion and her lips were parted as she struggled to catch her breath.

"Anna May," he whispered before he lowered his head. He kissed her lips over and over again with gentle loving kisses. He teased and taunted her until she let her dress slip to the floor. Cupping his head with her hand and pressing her body against his, she kissed him with all the passion she had inside her. Her tongue slipped between his parted lips to taste his passion. She groaned in protest when he ended the kiss.

"Yes," she replied breathlessly.

"Ric, don't stahh ...." Her soft moan echoed as he kissed her neck, her shoulder, the soft swell of her breast.

"I won't," he said unhooking her bra and peeling away the satin material. Leaning forward, he traced her nipple with his tongue. Her moans grew more frantic when he kneeled before her, forging a trail of kisses down her chest and stomach.

His body was on fire and her moans were as arousing as her touch. He rubbed his cheek against her belly. "Do you like this?" he whispered.

"How about this?" He felt her stiffen as he touched her belly button with his tongue.

Her sob was all the answer he needed. He kissed her stomach again, then rose to his feet. Bending down, he lifted her in his arms and carried her to his bed.

Ric stared into the darkness of the night. There was no need for him to close his eyes. Thick drapes prevented light from entering the bedroom. He was tired and he should have been.

He'd turned to Anna May over and over again during the night. It was as if he couldn't get enough of her, and making love to her had left his body completely satisfied. But what she'd said about family kept niggling away in the back of his mind, keeping him awake.

For as long as he could remember, family meant betrayal. It meant being at the mercy of someone else's whims, yet tonight Anna May had accomplished what neither his aunt and uncle nor his acquaintances had been able to do. She'd challenged and shaken his perception of family and control. She'd dropped what she was doing to have dinner with one of his clients. She'd been there for him when she had obligation to do so. Behaving exactly the opposite of what he'd come to expect from family. Instead, she'd done what she'd always done. Been his friend.

But she was more than his friend, she reminded him that she was family now. Should he believe that she would never betray him like his family had done in the past? He'd known her for almost twenty years, and in that time she'd never done anything to make him doubt her. He trusted her with his life, but could he trust her with his very heart? His soul?

Chapter Eleven

The next two weeks Ric worked long hours at his office. While the deal with J.V. Dickerson was coming to a close, two other projects required his attention. In the past the long hours wouldn't have bothered him, but he found himself looking at his clock at various times during the day, eager to go home—to be with his wife.

His impression of Anna May had changed. She was still his best friend, but as a wife she was warm and caring. He never realized how much he looked forward to having dinner with her after a long day. Although she'd eaten her dinner earlier, she would sit at the table with him and ask how his day went, sharing amusing stories from her office. His life had been so quiet before she came to live with him. Now he'd grown accustomed to the sound of music playing while she relaxed in the den reading a book, the sight of her perfume bottle next to his aftershave lotion, and her hurried dash around the bedroom as she dressed for work each morning.

As he made the long drive from his office to his home, he wondered how he would handle the tomb-like quiet when she left. She would leave despite the fact that she'd left her mark on nearly every room in the house. She would leave and he didn't want her to go.

A sliver of moonlight shone through the bare limbs of the pecan trees that lined either side of the narrow lane leading to his home. His home. He no longer had just a house. He had someone who cared about him. Anna May had made his house a home.

He was concerned when he entered his home. It was quiet. Anna May liked to have noise in the house when she was alone.

"Anna May," he called out as he walked from the kitchen to the den. Silence was his only response. The tension in his body subsided when he entered the room. She lay asleep on the sofa, covered with a patchwork quilt he recognized as a gift from her grandmother. He glanced at the clock on the mantel. It was nine o'clock.

She must be really tired, he thought, as he looked at her. Her sleep wasn't peaceful if the frown on her face was any indication. He touched her shoulder gently and said, "Anna May."

Slowly she opened her eyes. They were red and puffy as if she'd been crying.

"Oh, hi," she said slurring her words.

He frowned when he saw her wince as she sat up. "What's wrong?" he asked.

"I don't feel good. My period started today."

"Oh," he said as varying emotions made their way to the surface. He felt relieved that she wasn't pregnant, and they'd have to make love again to create a child. However the sight of her pain made him wish he could make it disappear. "Can I get you anything? An aspirin?"

She shook her head. "No, I took my prescription earlier this evening. It makes me sleepy."

"Why don't you go to bed?" he said watching her eyes slowly drift closed.

"Okay," she said without moving.

"Anna May, do you need help? Can you make it up the stairs?"

With seemingly great difficulty, she opened her eyes again. "I can make it up the stairs." Moving the quilt to the side, she slowly rose from the sofa. She gasped in pain when she tried to stand up straight.

"The hell you can," he said as she stood slightly bent at the waist with her hand over her stomach. He took off his suit jacket and laid it on the sofa. Sliding his arms beneath her knees and her shoulders, he lifted her in his arms.

"I'm too heavy for you," she protested, her voice heavy with sleep.

"No, you're not. You're just right," he said as he walked out of the room.

She'd fallen asleep before he reached the bedroom. He laid her gently on the bed, then placed the cover over her. She turned on her side with her knees bent. A faint line formed between her brows. Sitting on the bed, he gently traced the line before leaning down to kiss her brow. She turned into his touch and her frown disappeared. Stroking her cheek, he listened to the steady cadence of her breathing.

Was she going to be in this much pain every month? Why didn't the medicine stop the pain? he wondered as he watched her sleep. He tried to remember what she'd told him about her condition, but he didn't remember her mentioning anything about being in pain. His jaw tightened with determination. He was definitely going to find out more about her condition. Stroking her cheek one last time, he rose to his feet and noticed a brown medicine bottle on the nightstand. He picked it up and read the label before returning the bottle to the nightstand. According to the instructions, she'd take another pill sometime tonight. He walked downstairs to the kitchen and filled a glass with cold water. He'd planned on spending an hour working in his office, but he wasn't going to work tonight. Anna May needed him tonight, and he was going to be there for her. With the glass of water in his hand, he turned out the lights in the kitchen and walked up the stairs.

A dull, throbbing pain in her abdomen awakened her. Anna May opened her eyes slowly. Pain was no stranger to her during this time. Relief would come within minutes after she took her medication. But there was no medication for the pain in her heart.

She wasn't pregnant.

She knew the chances of getting pregnant so early in her marriage were slim, but she'd hoped and prayed she would beat the odds. She hadn't. Slowly she sat up, then groped for the prescription in the darkness.

"Turn on the light," Ric said. He voice was deep and rough from sleep.

"I didn't mean to wake you," she said and turned on the lamp.

"It's all right," he said as he rubbed his eyes. "How do you feel?"

"I'll feel better when I take this," she said opening the childproof cap.

"Are you in this much pain every month?"

Taking the pill then taking a sip of water, she replied, "No. I haven't felt this badly in a while. Stress plays a part of it, too. I guess the wedding and the move here was more stressful than I thought."

"Is there anything I can do for you?" he asked as she placed the glass on the nightstand.

Her heart melted at his words. Despite his Ice Man persona, he cares for me, she thought. But caring wasn't enough for her. She wanted his love. Her smile was tired but tender. "There's nothing you can do, but thank you for asking."

"Are you sure?"

She reached out and caressed his cheek. The rough stubble of his beard and the firmness of his jaw gave her comfort. "I'm sure."

Ric placed his hand over hers. Their gaze met, and a sense of union—two halves of a whole—filled her. Her physical pain, her disappointment at not being pregnant waned, and for a brief moment, she felt as if they'd truly come together as one.

He gently squeezed her hand before lifting it from his cheek. Drawing her forward, he kissed the palm of her hand, letting his lips linger as if he were savoring the tender moment. A comforting warmth flowed inside her.

"Good night, Anna May."

"Night," she replied and turned out the light. Darkness filled the room. Anna May pulled the covers over her shoulders and lay on her side. As she waited for sleep to overcome her, doubts and fears began to fester and multiply.

Could she have a child? What if despite everything, she didn't get pregnant?

She turned to the other side of the bed, trying to ignore the questions in her mind. But the questions kept coming. What would happen to their relationship? Could she pretend to be just his friend ever again?

No, she thought. She had reached the point of no return. Her feelings toward Ric had changed, grown to the point where she could no longer hide behind the mask of friendship. She knew what it was like to love him mentally and physically.

She turned back to her original position. So many things could go wrong. So many things were out of control in her life. What made her think this plan of hers would work? Was she fooling herself?

She stiffened in surprise when he put his arm over her waist and curved his body to hers.

"What's the matter?" he asked, his voice smooth and relaxed.

"I'm scared," she replied in a shaky tone.

"Scared of what?"

"What if I don't get pregnant? What if those tests were wrong and there *is* something wrong with me?"

He kissed her cheek tenderly as he caressed her arm and shoulder, then said softly, "There's nothing wrong with you. Didn't your doctor encourage you to have a child?"

"Yes," she whispered.

"Do you think your doctor would have said to have a child if you couldn't?"

"No," she said reluctantly. "But what if I don't. I can't imagine not having a child of my own. I know it's old-fashioned, but I want to be a mommy. I want to have a large family. Bake cookies. Go to Little League or cheerleading practice. Sometimes when I'm baby-sitting Noriah, I pretend she's my little girl, and I don't really want her to go home when Marianne comes to take her home."

"Give it time. It will happen." He squeezed her shoulder in reassurance.

"I hope so."

"Hey, you're not giving up, are you?" he drawled, pressing his lips to her temple. "We've just started. Don't you know that practice makes perfect?"

"I know but . . ." Her tone filled with doubt.

"None of that. It'll happen. You'll see," he said resting his chin lightly on the crown of her head.

Anna May lay in his arms in silence, wanting desperately to believe him but fear, like a dark cloud on the horizon, cast a shadow of doubt on her hopes and dreams. She prayed for a miracle. She prayed for a family of her own.

"The city of Atlanta awarded their bid today. Adam Wilson's company lost the bid," Warren Morgan said as he looked through the stack of papers in front of him.

From the opposite side of the conference table, Ric listened to Morgan's announcement in silence. The weak winter sun broke through the clouds, sending beams of pale sunshine through Ric's office.

The joy and triumph Ric expected to feel just wasn't there. He had the power to destroy his stepfather's company, and if Evan Wilson was still president, Ric wouldn't hesitate to do it. But from the information he'd gathered on his brother, Adam's style of management was nothing like his father's.

"That puts Wilson in a rough spot. Without that bid, it's only a matter of months before he's out of business," Ric said.

"True," Morgan agreed. "But he's generated more revenue since he's taken over the company than was raised in the past two years. If he had taken over a year earlier, he'd be making record profits. Adam Wilson is good—and with our backing, he could be great."

"Being good isn't going to help his company. If he doesn't get our backing, he'll be forced to shut down."

Morgan placed the papers he was holding on the table, then leaned back in his chair. "I thought we were buying his company. Have you changed your mind?"

"I'm going to buy Wilson and Wilson," he said with conviction. "The question is when."

"When? Are you thinking about waiting until he goes under before you buy the company?"

"That is an option."

"Why? Wilson's proposal is fair. If you bought him out now, you'd spend about the same amount as you would when he goes bankrupt, and the employees of Wilson and Wilson would probably stay now. If you wait, some of the best employees might look for another place to work."

"There's no guarantee they'll stay after I buy the company, either."

Morgan studied his employer. "You've made your decision already."

"Send a letter to Adam Wilson. Tell him the Justice Company has declined his proposal," Ric said.

Morgan folded his arms, and the pristine white cotton shirt stretched tightly across his chest. "I don't get it, Justice. If it was Jamison we were talking about, I'd agree to wait, but Wilson is a smart businessman, and he has the potential to do excellent work and earn millions for the company. I think you're making a mistake on this one."

"We'll see. What's next?" Ric replied.

Realizing he'd come to a brick wall, Morgan dropped the subject. "That's all I have for now on Wilson. I've heard Jamison is getting nervous now that we've backed out of buying his company."

"Jamison should be nervous. If we found out he embezzled funds, then criminal charges should be in store for him soon," Ric said.

"His stockholders are dumping their shares on the market, and there are rumors out that the remaining stockholders plan to audit the finances of the company. Jamison wasn't happy when we started questioning his company's accounting practices."

"I'm glad we're not in that mess," Ric said.

"We may not be completely out of it because we were negotiating to purchase his company. It's a case of guilt by association. The legal department has copies of every piece of documentation we've received and sent to Jamison. Any additional letters need to go through legal first. I have a feeling we're going to have to prove we're not involved with Jamison. Jamison seems to be the type to take people with him if he's going down. I wouldn't put it past him to try to get us involved with his dirty dealings."

"Keep me posted on it, and keep me posted on Wilson, too."

"Of course. I still think you're making a mistake

by not accepting Wilson's proposal," Morgan said as he gathered the papers in front of him.

Ric smiled then said, "Let's agree to disagree on this one, Morgan."

Morgan rose from his chair. "Would you care to make a small wager on Wilson and Wilson? If I remember correctly, the last time we agreed to disagree, I won the bet."

"That was sheer luck," Ric said as he stood.

"I prefer to think of it as skill. Your box at the Dome is first class."

Ric raised a single brow. He'd wagered and lost his box seats for three Atlanta Falcons home football games the last time they disagreed. Watching the Falcons play football in the Dome was one of the few indulgences he allowed himself. Missing those last three games had been difficult. "I'm glad you enjoyed the seats, but they're useless now that football season is over. Besides, what is there to bet on? Wilson is going to be mad when I buy his company."

"True. But it would have been nice to get your tickets to the Hawks games," Morgan replied as he walked to the door.

"Better luck next time," Ric said.

Morgan opened the door. "Not luck, skill," he said then walked out, closing the door behind him.

Ric walked to his desk. The corners of his lips curved slightly. Morgan could afford to buy box seats in each city that had a professional football team, but it was the thrill of winning using his own skills, and not money, that motivated him. Those traits were perfect for his position as senior business manager.

They had disagreed on a few occasions, and over the years, they'd come to respect each other's opinion. Compromise was usually how they resolved the difference of opinion. However, he couldn't compromise on the subject of Wilson and Wilson. So much of his life had been shaped by decisions made by Evan Wilson. Now it was time he shaped Evan Wilson's life.

"Mr. Justice?" Mrs. Jones called from her position in the doorway of his office.

"Yes," Ric answered, placing his pen on the desk. His eyes widened in surprise when he saw the carefully wrapped gift in her arms. Another secretary stood behind her also bearing gifts.

"The employees wanted to get you and your new wife a wedding gift," Mrs. Jones said.

"That wasn't necessary," he said as the women placed the boxes on his desk.

"We know it's not necessary, but we wanted to," the other woman said.

"Thank you," he said feeling slightly uncomfortable accepting gifts from his employees.

"Don't open them now," Mrs. Jones said. "Take them home so that you and your wife can open them together."

"I'll do that," he replied.

"Well, have a good evening, Mr. Justice. We'll see you tomorrow." The women walked out of his office.

Ric looked at the gifts on his desk. He could almost see the expression on Anna May's face when he brought them home. Her brown eyes would light up with excitement like they had a few weeks ago when they were married.

Although he felt uncomfortable receiving gifts from his employees, he hoped they would take her mind off the pain she was in. Last night for the first time, he'd seen firsthand how much pain she suffered. How she'd kept that from him all these years, he didn't know. He thought he'd known almost everything about Anna May, but he realized he'd only seen a part of the total woman.

He glanced at his watch. If he left his office now, he could beat the traffic. Ric cleared his desk, gathered the gifts, and walked out of his office. Mrs. Jones looked up from her computer when he stopped at her desk.

"I'm going home now. Thank you again for the gifts."

She raised her brow in surprise. "You're welcome. I hope Mrs. Justice enjoys them."

With a nod Ric strode out of the office and headed home.

Music greeted him as he entered the kitchen. Ric hoped this meant Anna May was feeling better. He placed the gifts on the dinette table ready to go search for his wife when she walked in. Her cream silk blouse molded to her soft form, and the navy skirt hugged her hips. Her business image was shattered when he noticed the bright pink polish on her toenails.

"Oh, you're home early," she said.

"What good is being the boss if you can't come home early every once in a while? I didn't think you were going to work today," he said as he studied her face for signs of pain.

She waved away his concern. "I felt better, so I went to the office. What's this?" she asked pointing to the boxes on the table.

"Wedding gifts from my employees," Ric said.

Her eyes brightened with anticipation. "Oh, that was nice of them. Let's open them now."

"Go ahead," he said as he took off his jacket then leaned against the counter.

"Here. Read the card," she said giving him the small envelope.

Ric pushed away from the counter, draped his jacket over the chair, then took the envelope. "It says: *To Mr. and Mrs. Garrick Justice from the human resources department. Best wishes on your recent marriage.*"

Placing the card on the table, he watched as she literally tore into the gifts. Long, ragged strips of wrapping paper were removed in quick sucession. Within seconds, she'd opened the first gift.

"How pretty," she said removing the delicate figurine from the protective bubble wrap. The man and woman stood side by side dressed in their wedding garb. The primitive yet simplistic style of the piece was the mark of an internationally acclaimed African-American artist. "This will look perfect next to our wedding picture."

Ric studied the figurine. "It's too valuable to leave unprotected. We should put it somewhere safe."

"No, don't do that. We would never enjoy it if it's locked up someplace."

"We'd never enjoy it if it's broken," he replied.

"Why don't I move our wedding picture from the end table in the living room to the mantel in the den. The statue would be less likely to be knocked over if it's on a mantel than the end table."

"I don't see how the mantel is any safer than the table. The statue should be behind glass somewhere, protected."

"Your car is more valuable, and you don't put it behind glass."

"That's different."

"How?"

"My car is a tool. A means to an end. The statue is decorative."

"The statue is like a tool. It builds memories and evokes feelings. Your car gets you from point A to point B. Art like this statue takes you from emotion to emotion. I think the people in your office gave us this gift so we could enjoy it, not hide it."

Ric held up his hands in surrender. "All right, we'll keep it in the den."

"Good," she said. Anna May set the statue on the table and picked up the next gift. After she removed the wrapping paper and opened the box, she smiled. "I think this is for you."

It was a gift certificate for the local do-it-yourself store and a Honey-Do List notepad. Anna May opened the card. "It's from the security guards," she said.

"I always liked those guys," he said as he held the gift certificate.

"Why don't you buy stock in the store? You're in there all the time."

"I've got stock already," he replied.

She smiled. "I should have known you would."

"I know a good company when I see one."

"And I know good people. The gifts are really nice, Ric. I'd like to personally thank them," she said.

"Why don't we have lunch one day this week, then I can introduce you to everybody."

Anna May rubbed her lower back in an attempt to ease the tension. "That sounds good."

"Does your back hurt?"

"It doesn't hurt exactly—my muscles are tight. It will go away by tomorrow."

"Do you want a back rub? It might help," he added when he noticed her skeptical expression.

"It might hurt."

"Just try it. If it hurts, I'll stop."

She thought about it for a few seconds, then shrugged her shoulders. "Okay, give it a try."

"Let's go to the den. I need you to lie on your stomach," he said.

"This isn't sounding good, Ric. My stomach hurts," she replied as she stood.

Ric stood beside her. "If it hurts you to lie on your stomach, then I won't give you a back rub."

"Okay."

The warmth of the fire in the fireplace filled the den. Pictures of her family were scattered around the room, and her knickknacks seemed to have a spot on every available surface.

She stretched out on the sofa with her cheek resting on her folded arms.

"How do you feel? Does that hurt?" Ric asked.

"I'm okay."

He kneeled on the floor beside the sofa. Slowly he messaged her shoulders, using the tips of his fingers and the palms of his hands to soothe and release the tension. Anna May felt the warmth of his hand through her thin silk blouse. "Ah," she moaned as he unraveled the knot of tension between her shoulders.

His hands became still. "Did that hurt? Do you want me to stop?" he asked.

"No, don't stop. It feels good."

He smiled then continued to stroke her taut muscles. Her eyelids fluttered then closed when he reached the small of her back. No drug could make her feel the way she felt at this very moment. Cherished, relaxed, and if she let herself dream, she felt loved.

Chapter Twelve

Anna May slowly opened her eyes. Still groggy from the medication, she wondered why she was on the couch. The dull ache in her stomach reminded her.

She wasn't pregnant.

No matter how many times she told herself not to expect to get pregnant so soon after her marriage, she had still wished, she had still prayed that she was pregnant. Her wish had gone unfulfilled.

The tap-tap of keystrokes drew her gaze to the desk in the corner of the room. Ric sat behind his desk. The soft glow of the lamp and his laptop illuminated his face. She would never grew tired of looking at him.

Her husband and her love.

The longer I'm with him, the more I fall in love with him, she thought, remembering the massage he'd given her. Pushing aside the blanket, a blanket he covered her with while she slept, she sat up on the couch.

Whatever was on the computer enthralled him. With his elbow on the desk, he rested his head in his hand and stared intently at the computer screen.

"What are you doing?" she asked brushing her fingers through her hair.

Ric looked up from the computer screen. "Surfing the Net for information on your condition."

"Oh. What did you find?" she asked.

He shrugged his shoulders. "Not much more than what you told me. I wish you didn't have to go through this. I wish you weren't in pain."

She felt his concern for her and treasured his caring feeling for her. If only he loved her. "Ric, I go through this every month. I'm fine. Really."

"I've never seen you like this."

"Why would you? When I didn't feel well, I usually stayed at home."

"I don't like it," he said. He rose to his feet and joined her on the couch. "Is having a baby worth the pain you're going through? We could adopt. You don't have to go through this."

Anna May bowed her head and closed her eyes, fighting the tears which threatened to fall. "It's worth it to me. I've always wanted children, you know that. If I had my way, I'd have a house full. But I don't think I'll have that option. A little pain is worth the chance to have a child."

He cupped her face in his hands and gazed into her eyes, his brown eyes filled with concern. "Then I'll do everything in my power to give you a child."

A single tear escaped and rolled down her cheek.

"Hey, hey—none of that," he said wiping away the tear with the pad of his thumb. When two more tears rolled down her cheek, he said, "Come on, Anna May. Don't cry."

She sniffled as the tears continued to fall.

"You know. If you keep this up, I'm gonna have to change my shirt, and you know what happened the last time I did."

Anna May's laugh sounded more like a sob. She had cried in Ric's arms when she learned the boy she was dating had asked her out only as a part of his fraternity initiation. Ric walked her to her dorm room, then told her he'd be back after he changed his shirt. Instead, he went to her date's dorm room and beat him up. Ric returned to her room wearing a clean shirt and sporting a black eye. When she asked how he got the black eye, he told her he'd run into something. It was a few days later when she'd crossed paths with her former date—his lower lip was cut, and dark bruises ringed his eyes. He made a U-turn when he saw her.

"No, I wouldn't want that to happen," she replied.

"Good," he said wiping away her tears and then releasing his hold on her.

She brushed away the remaining moisture. "I think I'll turn in for the night."

"Tired?" he asked.

She nodded her head. "Still groggy from the medication."

"Can you stay awake for a little while longer?"

"I guess. Why?"

"Your mother called while you were sleeping."

"Mom? What did she want?" Anna May asked.

"I don't know. She wants you to call her."

Anna May glanced at the clock over the mantel. The three-hour time difference meant it was seven o'clock in California. "I guess I'd better see what Mom wants," she said. She came to her feet and straightened gingerly. The medication helped ease the pain but didn't completely dull it. She walked to his desk and picked up the telephone.

"Hi Mom," she said cheerfully.

"How's my baby girl?" her mother asked.

"I'm fine."

"Anna May, I'm your mother. I know something's wrong. I can hear it in your voice. Now, tell Mama what's wrong."

Anna May smiled and sat in the chair. How her mother knew something was bothering her, she didn't know. It had to be an instinct parents developed, she thought wryly. "I can't pull anything over on you, can I?"

"No. Now what's wrong?"

She smiled at her mother's tenacity. Her mother never changed. Her smile faded as she remembered the reason for her earlier tears. "I'm not pregnant, Mom."

"Oh, baby girl," her mother said softly, conveying her sadness over the telephone line. "I'm sorry."

"Yeah—me, too, Mom. Me, too."

"Well, don't give up. I had a hard time getting pregnant. Your father and I tried for almost a year before Steven came along."

A year. It seemed like a lifetime. A tremor of fear entered her voice. "I don't know if I have a year."

"It probably won't take that long for you to have a child. Doctors are discovering ways to help couples have children every day. Don't worry."

"I can't help but worry," Anna May said.

"Honey, you just started. Worry and stress won't help your condition. So stop it."

And that's that, she thought to herself. Anna May smiled at the resolve in her mother's voice. "Yes, ma'am."

"Anna May, don't sass me."

"I'm not sassing you, Mom," she said.

"Hmm. I called to find out when you're coming for James's birthday."

Christmas, Thanksgiving, birthdays were cause for every member of the Robinson family to meet at her parents' home. This Saturday was James's thirty-fifth birthday, and she wasn't going to miss it. "I pick up my ticket tomorrow, Mom. I'll call you with the details then."

"Ric is coming with you, isn't he?"

It was a good question. She'd actually forgotten to mention her upcoming travel plans to Ric. Anna May glanced at her husband's relaxed form on the couch. He'd picked up a magazine from the coffee table and appeared to be reading.

"Anna May?" her mother queried.

"Uhh. I'll have to get back to you on that, Mom."

"What's that supposed to mean? Either he's coming or he's not."

"Well, I don't know yet."

"You put Ric on the phone. He's a part of the family now and expected to be here like the rest of the family," her mother said.

"Uhh."

"Don't uhh me. Put Ric on the telephone."

"But, Mom——I need to talk to him first."

"You need to talk to him first? Anna May, you did tell him you were coming to California for the weekend, didn't you?"

"Not exactly."

She heard her mother's long-winded sigh. "You better tell him before Saturday."

"I'll do it as soon as I get off the phone."

"Is that a hint?"

"No."

"Hmm," her mother said skeptically. "Call me tomorrow with the information on your flight."

"I will, Mom."

They said their goodbyes, and Anna May hung up the telephone.

"What do you have to talk to me about?" Ric asked.

Anna May looked across the room. Ric sat on the couch reading a magazine. "Were you listening to my conversation?"

Ric closed the magazine and put it on the coffee table. "It's hard not to hear your conversation when I'm sitting less than fifteen feet away."

"That was rude."

"If you wanted privacy, you could have gone into another room. What do you have to talk to me about?"

"You know, you and my mother are beginning to sound a lot alike."

Ric raised a single brow. "My voice has a bit more bass than your mother's."

She shook her head. "I need to talk to you about this weekend."

"What about this weekend?"

"Saturday is James's thirty-fifth birthday. We've planned a big party for him at my parents' house."

Ric folded his arms and looked at her suspiciously."Are you trying to tell me you're going to California in two days?"

Anna May looked at him with a hopeful expression. She wanted him to be with her and her family. The birthday party was the perfect time to show him a loving family. He'd turned down her offers to join her and her family so many times over the years, she'd finally stopped inviting him.

This time was different.

Now more than ever, he needed to attend this party. "I was thinking maybe we could both go."

He frowned. "Two days isn't a lot of notice."

"I know. I've been putting off telling you about the party because I was afraid you wouldn't come with me. I *want* you to come with me, Ric. The party's all set, and all you have to do is show up. It will be fun."

He studied her from across the room.

She waited in anxious silence as he thought it over. Her heart raced.

Finally he said, "When do we leave?"

The following morning . . .

Adam Wilson placed the letter on his desk. He didn't have to read it again. He knew what it said.

Thanks, but no thanks.

He leaned back in his chair and closed his eyes. Failure was foreign to him. He'd always accomplished the goals he'd set for himself. This goal of bringing the company his grandfather started out of financial ruin seemed out of his reach. After his meeting with Ric Justice, he was confident Justice would agree with his plan. It was a good plan, profitable for both companies. And Justice had declined his offer.

In his current situation, he had nine months of revenue coming into his company. After that time Wilson and Wilson would close its doors. The hum of voices in the outer office drifted into his own. In nine months his employees would be out of a job. Nine months. His employees had welcomed his new ideas and had worked hard to cut costs to make the company more profitable. They didn't deserve to be put out on the street.

His options were crappy. He could lay off some of his employees and hope he could garner more business in the coming year to stay afloat. He could tell the employees to start looking for other jobs and hope he had enough employees to run the company, or he could try to find another source of income. But what person in their right mind would invest in a company as heavily in debt as his?

Justice hadn't.

"Hey, boy. What are you doing? Sleeping on the job?" His father's voice boomed in the office.

Adam opened his eyes and looked at his father. The man who shaped his life with heavy-handed discipline. The man that shaped Ric Justice's life with cruelty.

"No. What are you doing here?"

His father made himself comfortable in a chair facing his desk. "What? Can't I come by to see my son?" his father asked with an air of innocence.

"I know you, Dad. What do you want?" Adam rubbed his jaw.

His father's gaze was piercing and direct. At one time in his life, that stare would have been enough to unnerve him, but years of experience in the business world had made him strong. His father no longer had the power to disturb him.

Evan Wilson blinked. "I just wanted to know how things were going. I've owned this company for thirty years. It's hard to let it go completely, even with you running things."

"You knew that before you retired."

"I didn't expect my own son to kick me out. I

thought I had at least a year of transition to retired life."

"You agreed to the terms of the buyout, Dad. At the time you and I agreed it would be best if you stepped out of the picture. Our styles of management are totally incompatible."

Evan rose. "I made this company what it is today."

"A company so deep in debt that our stockholders are dumping our shares," Adam replied.

"And what are you doing? Trying to sell the company to Justice," Evan said in disgust. "You're giving up at the first sign of trouble. I never gave up on this company. I took the good times with the bad."

"Is that why you embezzled three quarters of a million dollars? Because you were taking the good times with the bad?"

Adam watched as blood drained from his father's face. "I . . . I don't know what you're talking about," Evan said.

"I'm talking about the money you stole from the company last year. Did you think I wouldn't find out, or didn't you care?"

"I never took anything that wasn't mine from this company. If money is missing, you should be finding out who took it," Evan blustered.

"I know you took the money. I know how you moved it around from account to account, and I even know you have it tucked away in several Caribbean bank accounts."

The tense silence stretched in the room. "How did you find out?" his father asked.

"Does it matter?"

"No. It doesn't matter because you won't do anything about it."

Adam met his father's gaze. "You're right. I'm not going to do anything about it."

Evan smiled mockingly and walked to the door, confidence in his stride.

Waiting until his father reached the doorway, he said in a calm, soft voice, "Dad, I know about the fire."

Evan Wilson drove his late-model Lexus through the busy streets of downtown Atlanta. Traffic was moderate at two o'clock, which worked in his favor because his mind wasn't on driving. How had Adam found out about the bank accounts? And what the hell did he mean with that cryptic statement, "I know about the fire." Nobody knew he'd deliberately burned down his own company. The fire department had never suspected arson, and the insurance company paid him dearly to rebuild. How had Adam found out? No, he couldn't know.

The boy was getting too big for his britches. I should have made him come to work for me right out of college. Adam should have been making money for the family business instead of making all that money for that two-bit engineering firm, Evan thought. His lips tightened with anger when he thought of all the money he could have made, all the power that came with it. He'd still be in change now, and he could have made life hell for Ric Justice. Instead, his boy was trying to sell his company to Justice.

Evan's hand clenched on the steering wheel. He'd have to show them both who was in charge. Nobody messed with Evan Wilson. Nobody.

* * *

Anna May's father met them at the gate of Orange County International Airport.

"Daddy," she said, racing to the older man's side, then hugged and kissed him like she hadn't seen him in years instead of a few weeks. Ric followed at a more subdued pace. Ever wary of her father's reaction, he breathed an inward sigh of relief when her father returned her embrace.

Anna May had so much faith and confidence in her family, he thought. She would never think her family would betray her, but he knew from painful experience how badly family treated family. He'd agreed to come with her on this trip for that very reason. He wasn't about to let her family hurt her like his family had hurt him.

For the past two days Anna May had reassured him of the fun they would have at her brother's party. He had yet to attend one of her family's parties. In the past he made sure she received her birthday gift before the party. Birthday parties brought to mind vague childhood memories of balloons, cake, and a tall man making him laugh. Later, his aunt had shown him a picture his father had sent to her of him and his father wearing party hats. It was his fourth birthday. The year his father was killed.

"Come on, Ric."

Anna May's happy voice penetrated his memories and brought him back to the present. She and her father stood arm in arm waiting for him. "Hello, Mr. Robinson," he said when he reached the duo.

Mr. Robinson held out his hand. "How are you, Ric? How was the flight?"

"Fine, sir," he replied as he shook his hand.

"Good. Let's get you two to the house. Carolyn's probably pacing a hole in the floor. You know how excited she gets about these big parties," Mr. Robinson said.

"And you don't," Anna May said in a teasing tone.

"I can take them or leave them," her father said.

"Okay, then I'll stay at home on your next birthday," she said as they walked down the terminal.

Ric's muscles tensed at the frown on Mr. Robinson's face.

"I wouldn't go that far, baby girl. A man likes to have his children around on special occasions. It makes him feel alive."

"It also ensures you'll get a present," she said.

Mr. Robinson laughed. "That, too."

Ric let his muscles relax, when he realized he didn't need to protect her. He listened to their banter as they claimed their bags, left the airport, and on the ride to her parents' home in her father's late-model car, occasionally adding a comment from the backseat.

The banter didn't stop until they turned into the driveway of a Spanish-style house surrounded by palm trees. Before the car came to a stop, the front door opened and Mrs. Robinson walked out onto the porch.

"I told you she was pacing a hole in the floor," her father teased as he parked the car.

Anna May was out of the car in a flash. With arms opened wide, she ran to her mother.

"We'd better bring in the bags," her father said. "They'll be holed up together for a good hour."

Ric felt a sense of dread. He was going to be left with Anna May's father for an hour. Taking a look over his shoulder at his wife and mother-in-law, who were making their way to the front door, he hoped Anna May wouldn't leave him alone with her family an hour.

She left him for two hours and fifteen minutes. Ric was surrounded by her brothers, cousins, and uncles. He'd lost count of names an hour ago when he'd been introduced to relative number fifteen, a cousin, and his wife and two small children.

James's birthday party was more like a Robinson family reunion. Food from tacos to hot dogs to fried chicken abounded. Ric had yet to see a birthday cake, but brightly wrapped gifts covered the long folding table in the den where most of the family had gathered.

"Get away from my presents, Anna May," James said from across the room.

Ric watched his wife walk to the table and place the gift among the others. "You'd better be glad I didn't open it on the way here," she said.

He found himself laughing with the rest of the family at her remark. So far being with her family wasn't as miserable as he thought it would be. Most of the people knew who he was, and although he couldn't remember meeting most of them, they treated him fairly.

"How are you holding up?" Anna May asked when she reached his side.

Her brown eyes glowed with happiness. There among the noisy crowd of her family, Ric felt desire rise up within him. He wanted her. He wanted to taste her sweet lips, to hear the moans she made when she was aroused.

"Ric?"

"What?"

"Are you having a good time? You're not bored, are you?" she asked with a puzzled look on her face.

"No, I'm not bored."

"Good," she sighed in relief. "I didn't mean to leave you alone for so long, but Mom needed help."

"No problem. Your uncle has been filling me in on the Robinson family history."

"Which uncle?"

"That one," he said looking across the room.

Anna May followed his gaze. "Oh. Uncle Clyde. Take what he said to you with a grain of salt. Uncle Clyde tends to exaggerate."

He smiled. "You mean you aren't smart as a whip?"

"Uncle Clyde is a very wise man," she said solemnly.

A piercing whistle sounded in the room. "Listen up, everybody," Steven Jr. said. "It's time for the birthday boy to open his gifts. Good thing, too. I don't think Anna May or James could wait much longer."

"Hey," she said indignantly.

Steven Jr. ignored her. "Let's sing to my little brother so we can eat the chocolate cake Mom's been guarding like the crown jewels."

Ric joined in the very off-key rendition of the birthday song. When the song ended, he learned James wasn't much better than Anna May when it came to opening gifts. Within minutes the neatly wrapped gifts were reduced to scraps of paper on the floor. Watching in amusement as James opened the last gift, he put his arms around Anna May's shoulders. Her smile sent heat coursing through him.

Three days, he reminded himself. He had to wait for three more days to make love to his wife.

"Dad, how did you know I wanted this?" James's excited voice interrupted his thoughts. James held up a box with a familiar Black and Decker logo. Ric's opinion of Mr. Robinson increased. He had that same tool in his attic.

"I saw you looking at it when we were in the hardware store. I figured you could help me finish the room downstairs." Mr. Robinson laughed.

"Oh, no," Anna May said. "There goes Mr. Tooltime."

James smiled and opened the box. "Let's go try it out now."

"James Robinson," Mrs. Robinson said in a stern voice. "You put that thing back in the box. You're going to cut the cake and enjoy it."

"But—" James added.

Mrs. Robinson held up her hand. "In the kitchen for cake, young man."

Ric watched in amusement as James put away his tool.

"Don't worry, son," her father said putting his arm around his son's shoulder. "We'll go downstairs right after we finish the cake."

"Hmm," Mrs. Robinson replied.

They did exactly that. All the men of the family went downstairs.

"Come on, Ric," her father said. "You've got to see this."

He put down his half-eaten cake and followed the men downstairs. Insulation and Sheetrock lined the walls of the unfinished room. Ric felt instantly at ease among the chaos of construction.

"So this is why you told us to wear jeans, James?" one of the uncles asked.

"Yes. You don't know how much we've been looking forward to this. Mom is convinced we need a contractor to finish the room, but Dad and I can do it. We went to the Home Depot class last week," James said.

"Ha," Steven Jr. said. "That's what you said about putting up tile in my house. I had to hire somebody to redo your work."

"That was last year. All we have to do is lay the insulation and put up the Sheetrock," James interjected.

"Right, Mr. Tooltime," Steven Jr. scoffed.

"He's right," Ric said quietly and regretted he'd said anything when everyone looked at him.

"You know construction?" one of the cousins asked.

"Yes. I'm finishing my attic now," Ric answered.

"Let's get to it then," James said, hefting a roll of insulation to the far wall.

Within minutes and after a few instructions, the men had most of room insulated. Ric and Steven Jr. finished the wall they were working on and watched as the others completed their task.

"Good thing you were here. Dad and James would have messed up this room for sure."

Ric agreed, but he wasn't about to say it with Mr. Robinson a few feet away.

"I heard that," Mr. Robinson said. "See if we help you fix anything again."

"You promise?" Steven Jr. replied.

Ric joined in the laughter as father and son matched wits. For all the teasing and joking among her family, he could see that the Robinson family truly cared for each other. They weren't so bad. For a family.

Chapter Thirteen

"Are you going to buy it or stare at it forever?" Ric asked from his position behind the shopping cart. The farmers' market was filled this Monday night with shoppers buying exotic produce from around the world, and it seemed Anna May had to study each and every one of them before leaving.

He should have known a quick trip to the market wasn't possible for her. The last time they went to the grocery store, she had him there for an hour and a half.

She smiled at him in that patient way of hers. "I just want to make sure it's fresh."

How could she tell, he wondered to himself. The yellow bulb-shaped thing she was holding didn't look like something he wanted to eat. "What is that?"

She raised her brows in surprise. "Rutabaga."

"Oh. Are you going to get it or not?"

"Be patient," she said removing a clear plastic bag from the counter.

Patience he was learning wasn't his strong suit when it came to Anna May. When they flew home from California yesterday, all he wanted to do was spend time with his wife. The more he was around her, the more he wanted her.

And he had to wait.

A day. Twenty-four hours. It seemed like a lifetime. If he felt this way now, he wondered how he would feel when the baby came and she no longer needed him. He wasn't going to lie to himself. Once she had the child, her family, she wouldn't want him around. Family never wanted him. That was true. Ric remembered how much fun he had at her parents' home. They seemed to enjoy having him, and he'd felt a part of the Robinson family while helping to finish the room. Maybe he was wrong, he thought, as he watched Anna May place vegetables in the plastic bag. Maybe she wouldn't leave him once the baby came.

"Do you think this is enough?" she asked holding up the bag for his inspection.

"You're asking me? I didn't know what those were until a few minutes ago."

She shook her head and put the bag in the cart. "Never mind."

"What are you going to do with those anyway?" he asked as he followed her to the next pile of unrecognizable produce.

"Make a casserole," she said as he picked up a vegetable that looked like a root on steroids.

"Rutabaga casserole. Wonderful."

Her eyes widened, and she shook the root at him. "Ric, you've been eating my squash and rutabaga casserole for years."

"I have?"

"Yes," she said.

Ric breathed a sigh of relief when she put down the root and moved on to another pile of vegetables. He didn't want to think about what he'd been eating. Maybe he didn't want to know.

Anna May turned the corner and walked down another aisle. Things looked even worse on this aisle.

"Don't they have things like celery?" he asked.

"We're getting to it," she said placing another bag in the cart.

"How do you know what to do with this stuff anyway?" He looked at the item in her hand and frowned. "Shouldn't that be given a decent burial?"

"Ric," she laughed. "Leave the shopping to me and just push the cart."

"Yes, ma'am."

She smiled at him and melted his heart. "No, that's yes, dear."

She was his dear, he realized. He watched the teasing smile melt from her face as he touched her cheek. "Yes, dear," he said softly.

Surprise then desire flashed in her brown eyes, and he was sure the same emotions were reflected in his own. He lowered his head and touched his lips to hers. The kiss was soft, sweet, and short.

She pulled away from his embrace and glanced around in embarrassment. "We'd better finish," she said then turned and moved down the aisle.

Ric followed her with the cart. He felt dazed. In previous relationships he hadn't shown affection in public, and now in the middle of the largest farmers' market in Atlanta, he'd kissed his wife. He waited to feel embarrassment at his action, but he felt none. In fact, he felt darn good. He smiled and pushed the cart along. He was like the other men following their women around the maze of the market. He was a husband, spouse, a significant other. It wasn't a bad thing to be.

"Oh, hi," Anna May said.

His aunt and uncle made their way down the aisle. He was surprised to see them. Not that he knew their shopping habits, but they'd moved from Decatur to Stockbridge about an hour's drive away.

"Hello, how are you doing?" his aunt asked.

"Fine, and you?" Anna May said.

"We're doing okay," she said looking at him with an air of expectancy. That same look had sent him running for cover when he was a teenager. He didn't know what she wanted from him then, and it made him uncomfortable, restless, and eager to get out of her way.

They stood in silence. "Well, it was nice seeing you," his aunt said.

Anna May looked from him to his aunt, and her eyes pleaded with him. "Do you shop here often?"

"Betty makes a trip up here every two weeks to buy out the store," John Steward added in his slow south Georgia accent.

Ric watched as his aunt gave his uncle an irritated look. "I like to buy fresh vegetables, and I don't hear you complaining about the food at home," she said.

"They should build a sitting area for the men so they can wait until we finish shopping," Anna May said.

"Why don't you go shopping by yourself?" Ric asked. He knew he was in trouble when Anna May and his aunt frowned at him. His uncle John shook his head. He'd obviously committed some social error.

"Son," his uncle said. "That was the wrong thing to say."

Son. Uncle John had almost always called him son.

He felt no resentment at the name like he had when he was younger. What had happened to him? Had Uncle John changed, or was he the one who had changed?

His thoughts were interrupted by Anna May's elbow in his side. "Didn't you want to come to the market with me?"

"Yes, I did."

"Then why did you say I should have come by myself?" she asked.

"That's not what I meant," he said resisting the urge to rub his side. "I meant"—he stopped when his uncle shook his head once more—"never mind."

"We were about finished here. Would you join us for dinner?" his aunt said.

Anna May looked to him for an answer. Dinner with his aunt and uncle. Should he join them? His initial thought was to decline her offer, but he could see the hopeful expression on her face. What could it hurt? It was only dinner. "Sure," he said.

His aunt's smile was radiant, but it was Anna May's nod of approval that made him realize he'd made the right choice.

They dined at Mick's just off the Decatur Square. "I hope this place is okay? I didn't think to ask before we left the farmers' market," Uncle John said when they entered the restaurant.

"It's great," Anna May said.

The restaurant was fairly crowded, and they had to wait for a table. Anna May and Aunt Betty kept conversation going talking about friends in their old neighborhood.

"I saw Mrs. Davis not too long ago," Anna May said.

"Jewel Davis. How is she?"

"The same. Still as ornery as ever. She was complaining that the kids in the neighborhood were messing up her yard," Anna May said.

The older man laughed. "Remember when Ric mowed the lawn for the first time and accidentally mowed a part of her grass? I thought Jewel was going to have a heart attack right there on the spot. It was all I could do not to laugh in her face when she came running over."

"Poor Ric. He was terrified," his aunt added. "He had no idea she was all talk. I think for a long time he believed she really was going to take a strip off his hide like she said she was."

Ric listened in confusion. He didn't remember the incident that way. His uncle sounded like Anna May's father recounting his son's childhood antics, not the stern man he remembered. "I thought I was in serious trouble," he said.

"In trouble? No, you weren't in trouble. I wanted to take you out to celebrate," his uncle replied.

"You mowed the rest of lawn that day and always watched me mow the lawn from then on."

His uncle frowned. "I finished the job because Jewel would have followed you up and down the yard making sure you didn't cut a single blade of her precious grass. And I just liked sitting outside. I wasn't watching you mow the grass. Is that what you thought?"

"Yes, I thought you were going to send me back to my grandmother."

His uncle regarded him with a hint of sadness in his eyes. "Son, you couldn't be more wrong."

"We were so glad to have you move in with us. You were all I had left of my brother. We wouldn't have ever sent you to live with that woman again," his aunt said.

Ric studied the elderly couple. How could he have misjudged the situation? Maybe his perception had been skewed as a teenager. Maybe his aunt and uncle weren't as bad as he'd made them out to be. Maybe he'd been wrong about them like he'd been wrong about Anna May's family.

"Would anyone care for dessert?" their waiter asked breaking the solemn mood around the table.

They all declined and waited for the check.

"Thank you for inviting us to dinner," Anna May said.

"It was our pleasure," John said.

"Next time we'll pick a restaurant on your side of town," Ric said.

"We'd like that," his aunt said, her smile at odds with the tears in her eyes.

"It was nice of you to invite them to dinner next week," she said as he drove down the dimly lit expressway on their way home. She couldn't have been more proud of him, Anna May thought on the drive home. He could have ended the evening without offering an olive branch to his aunt and uncle, but he had been the one to initiate another meeting. It had meant so much to the older couple, particularly his aunt.

Ric made a noncommittal sound.

"Where do you think we should go for dinner?" she asked.

"I don't know," he said.

"Maybe I'll give your aunt a call and get some suggestions from her. Or . . ." She paused.

He glanced at her briefly before returning his attention to the road. "Or?"

"We could have them over for dinner. Nothing fancy, just plain food. What do you think?" She waited in anticipation for his answer. Dinner at a restaurant would be okay, but dinner at his home would be better. It would give them a chance to become closer. One step closer to bridging the gap with his family.

"Dinner at the house is fine with me," he said.

Anna May breathed a sigh of relief and gave a prayer of thanks. He didn't know it, but Ric was about to become a part of a loving family. Between her family and his aunt and uncle, he was going to learn the value of a loving family. All she had to do now was find his brother, but she didn't think it would be a problem. His aunt probably knew the whereabouts of his brother.

Slowly but surely, she'd show Ric the value of family, and hopefully he would learn to love her as his wife.

"So how long is Ric going to be out of town?" Janet asked after the waiter left the table.

"Five days," Anna May said glumly over the hum of the lunch crowd. The tiny restaurant in the middle of downtown was filled to capacity. It was known for its excellent food, but her mind wasn't on food. At ten thirty this morning, Ric called her at work to tell her he had to go out of town and he would probably be gone the entire week. After the days and nights of abstinence, she'd been looking forward to tonight. Tonight when she could be with her husband, but it wasn't to be.

"Don't be so down in the dumps. Think of it as five days of preparation," Janet said.

"Preparation?"

"Preparation for his return home," she said. "Pamper yourself, rest up, and make plans to seduce him while he's away. Send him a gift at his hotel or talk sexy to him on the telephone. It will make him want to come home soon."

"Janet, I'm afraid to ask how you know this."

Janet's bland expression was tempered by the mischievous twinkle in her eyes. "I never reveal my sources."

"You're a stockbroker, not a reporter." Anna May laughed.

"If the shoe fits," she said. "Tell me, how are things between you and Ric?"

"Things are okay. I didn't think I could love him more, but I do."

"That's good—and what about your plans to have a baby? How's that working?"

"Nothing's happened yet—" She stopped when Janet raised her eyebrows. "I mean I'm not pregnant."

"Oh." That one word conveyed her sadness. "Don't worry, you'll have a baby."

"I hope so."

"You will, but"—Janet paused then smiled wickedly—"enjoy making the baby. You've been waiting thirty-two long years for this. Enjoy it."

Anna May shook her head. "You're so crazy."

"No, I'm practical. Why would you pass up an opportunity to enjoy a choice, USDA prime, black male in your bed?"

Anna May raised a single brow. "Who said I'd pass up the opportunity?"

* * *

Later that evening as she curled up on the sofa in the den, the telephone rang.

"Hello?"

"Hi." His voice was like molten chocolate over the telephone line. "I got the flowers. Thanks."

It had taken her an hour to find a florist willing to deliver five calla lilies and a note which said, *Five days and counting. Come home soon.* to his hotel room in Los Angeles. She'd pretended not to hear the florist's chuckle on the telephone. Sending him flowers seemed like a good idea at the time, but now she was beginning to think it was hokey.

"I hope you like them," she said softly.

"I like them, but I'd like them even better if I was home. I'm sorry I had to leave, but this was an emergency. I had to handle this or else I'd have sent someone else."

"I understand. How was the meeting?"

He sighed in frustration. "About as bad as I thought it would be. I will definitely be here the whole five days trying to straighten out this mess."

"Oh." Her disappointment clear in her voice.

"Yes—oh."

"Well, when you're in your meetings, just remember this—I have a lot of gifts you haven't seen from my bridal shower."

"Anna May, are you flirting with me?" he asked in surprise.

"No, I'm trying to seduce you. Is it working?"

His laugh was low, deep, and sexy. "You'll have to wait until I come back to find out."

"Is that a challenge, Garrick?" she asked with a smile.

"You could say that, Anna May," was his amused reply.

"You're on."

"Are you sure? You know I've had a bit more experience in this area than you," he said, making each word sound like a caress.

"Don't be so conceited."

"I'm not conceited. I'm just sure of my abilities."

"We'll see how sure you are of your abilities when you get home," she said mockingly.

"No, *you'll* see how sure I am of my abilities when I get home."

"Okay. Ric?"

"Yes?"

"Hurry home."

Anna May was paid to read the newspaper. Every business day, she and her co-workers read international, national, and local newspapers. It was their job to clip news articles on their company and their competitors. It was in the local Atlanta business paper that she saw the brief article mentioning Ric and his brother, Adam Wilson. According to the article, Wilson and Wilson's stock price had reached an all-time low. The major reasons for the drop in prices were a failure to win a city of Atlanta bid and the failure to establish a partnership with the Justice Company. The reporter ended the article with a prediction that Wilson and Wilson would be in dire circumstances by the end of the year if they didn't win a major contract soon.

She folded the paper and placed it on her desk.

Surely Ric wouldn't let his brother's company go under? She couldn't imagine allowing either of her brothers to struggle and not offering assistance. But Ric hadn't been raised to help family. Leaning back in her chair, she wondered what if anything she should do? Should she stay out of it? After all, it was Ric's business. He knew what was best for his company.

In her heart of hearts, she knew she couldn't stand back and do nothing. As far as she was concerned, Adam Wilson was family by marriage. There had to be some way to help him, she thought.

With a snap of her fingers, she said, "Janet." As a stockbroker, Janet had access to various avenues of corporate information, and she could also get information from other stockbrokers on Adam Wilson's company.

She placed the call to Janet.

"Janet Hill speaking."

"Janet, it's Anna May."

"Anna May. Anna May? The name sounds familiar. I had a friend named Anna May once. But she got married a few weeks ago and fell off the face of the earth."

"Janet," she cried.

"Well, I guess I should give you a break since you're still a newlywed," Janet said dryly.

"Friends. They just don't make them like they used to."

"Ha! Give me a break."

Anna May laughed. Janet could always make her laugh with her dry humor. She was going to have to invite the Ladies' Club over soon. There was a hint of seriousness in Janet's comment about her dropping off the face of the earth. She didn't want her girlfriends to feel as if she was ignoring them. Maybe she would have them over during the week while Ric was still out of town. Ric was the reason she'd called Janet in the first place.

"Janet, I've got a favor to ask."

"What is it?"

"What do you know about an Atlanta-based company called Wilson and Wilson?"

"It doesn't ring a bell. Why? Are you interested in buying stock?"

Anna May was reluctant to tell her the real reason she wanted the information about Wilson and Wilson. Janet was her friend, and she could trust her with anything—but this was something she had to work through on her own for now. "I don't know yet. Could you find out what you can on the company and get back to me as soon as possible?"

"Sure, I'll ask around. I'm sure someone else here knows about them," Janet said, her voice filled with curiosity.

"I appreciate it."

They talked for ten minutes before the demands of their jobs forced them to end the call. Anna May reached for the newspaper. She hoped Janet uncovered information about Adam Wilson as well as his company. She wanted to know more about Ric's little brother, and she hoped he was a good man. Ric needed his family. Her family would be there for him, but he needed and deserved to know his brother. And if she could make it possible, she would.

A large brown box sat on Anna May's desk when she returned from lunch later that afternoon. She'd eaten lunch in the small cafeteria in the building rather than join a few of her co-workers who'd braved the arcticlike temperatures outside for a Varsity hamburger. Anna May smiled in delight when she saw the return address. It was the address of Ric's hotel in Los Angeles. Ric hadn't wasted any time. He had to have bought the gift last night and had it sent overnight, she thought. She opened her desk drawer and removed a pair of scissors. With more speed than grace, she opened the cardboard box. Small, colorful bottles of scented oils and candles created a rainbow of colors among the white Styrofoam packing materials. The assortment of smells blended together and brought to mind a rich botanical garden in full bloom. She took a deep breath to savor the sweet scent.

She could feel her muscles relax as the fragrance began to fill her office. Ric. She had to give it to him. The gift certainly melted her heart, and he knew she was a sucker for pretty things. She removed a blue bottle, and her gaze moved to a folded sheet of paper with her name printed on the front. She put the bottle in the box and read the note. *To remind you of our wedding night. Ric.*

"Like I'm going to forget," she muttered to herself as she sat in her chair. With a single sentence, he'd made her think of the most wonderful night of her life. Warmth spread through her as she remembered each touch, each sight, and each sound of that night. One thing would have made the night perfect: if Ric told her he loved her.

She was working on it. He wouldn't let himself love anyone, and until he made peace with his family, she knew he couldn't really love her. Ric's past was the bridge that led to his future. He'd taken the first step when he invited his aunt and uncle to dinner. Anna

May was going to make sure he kept moving in the right direction and developed a relationship with his brother. Janet had called her just before lunch. From what Janet had learned about Wilson and Wilson and Adam Wilson, Anna May knew she had to help. Adam seemed a lot like Ric. Tough, driven, and smart. She didn't know why Ric refused to help him. It couldn't be for the reason Janet suggested. Ric wouldn't wait until his brother's company was on the brink of bankruptcy before buying the company.

She wouldn't believe it.

The more she thought about Adam Wilson, the more she wanted to know about his mother. Ric's mother. What kind of woman left one son and kept another?

There was one person who could answer her question. Flipping the pages of her black leather Daytimer, she found the Stewards' telephone number. She picked up the handset and dialed the number. Mr. Steward's prerecorded voice on their answering machine requested her name, number, and a brief message. Anna May left a message for Mrs. Steward, hoping to hear from her by the end of the day. She didn't hear from Mrs. Steward until the following week when they'd returned from their vacation.

Ric entered his hotel room at eight o'clock that evening. Setting his leather briefcase on the desk, he loosened his tie and unbuttoned the top button of his shirt.

This business trip seemed more troublesome than any other trip he'd made. The problems he faced with the small Los Angeles-based engineering firm weren't unique. What had changed was his attitude.

He still wanted to solve the problems with the company, but now he wanted the problems solved quickly and without much fuss. What he wanted was to go home to his wife.

Shedding the navy double-breasted suit jacket, he draped it over the back of a chair, then reached for the telephone. The three-hour time difference would make it eleven o'clock in Atlanta. He remembered how tired she'd been when he'd left and hoped she wasn't in bed. She answered on the first ring.

"Hello." Her voice sounded a little breathless. It sounded sexy.

"Hi," he said as he sat down on the bed. Until he heard her voice, he hadn't realized just how much he'd missed her. "Did I wake you?"

"No. I was hoping you'd call. How's it going?"

"Slow," he replied. "Very, very slow."

"I'm sorry."

"Yeah—me, too. How are you doing? Are you feeling okay?"

"I'm fine. Oh, and I got your package. It was very nice," she said grudgingly.

He smiled at her tone of voice. "I'm glad you like it. You're pretty easy to please when it comes to gifts."

"What do you mean?"

"You like anything colorful, bright, and different like that red sweater of yours. You could use that sweater as a beacon it's so bright, and it suits you."

"I like my sweater. It's cheery," she said.

He liked the sweater, too. The soft wool molded to her breasts like a lover's hands. He'd had many a daydream about removing that sweater. "I like it, too," he said.

They talked for thirty minutes. When Anna May

could no longer hold back a yawn, he said, "I better
let you get some sleep."

"I guess I'm more tired than I realized," she said.

"Good night, Anna May."

"Good night, Ric. Hurry home."

Chapter Fourteen

On Friday Anna May left her office an hour earlier than her normal time of six thirty, among joking remarks from her co-workers on impatient newlyweds. She didn't mind their jokes. Ric was coming home today, and she wanted everything just right for his return. His flight was due to land in an hour. When she arrived home, she taped a note on the door which lead to the garage, took a shower, changed into one of her silky teddies, and lit the scented candles he'd given her, which she placed around the bedroom. Everything was ready. The only thing missing was Ric.

Nervously she rearranged the candleholders on the nightstand. Five days had seemed like an eternity to be away from him. Now that the time was near for his return, she could hardly wait. When she realized she'd placed the candleholders in the exact same position she'd had them before, she forced herself to sit down on the bed. Nervously she fingered the ring Ric had given her years ago. She let her gaze wander around the bedroom. The dim candlelight provided a warm glow to the room and an air of romance. The light scent of jasmine was provided by the burning candles.

Tonight would be a night to remember. Never had she realized how sexy it was just to talk to him. Their telephone bill was going to be huge. They'd talked to each other on the telephone until they could barely remain awake. It was as if they couldn't get enough of the other's company. She knew she couldn't get enough of his. The distance between them had made her realize how much she cherished Ric's company.

It also made her realize how much she loved him.

She nearly jumped off the bed when she saw the flash of car lights out of the window. It took nearly all her self-control to stay in the bedroom and not run downstairs to greet him. He would find her note soon. She didn't have long to wait. Her heart raced as she listened to the rapid footsteps on the stairs.

Then he was there. Standing in the doorway like a king surveying his dominion, holding her note in his hand. His gaze like a physical caress touched and moved her.

"I see you found my note," she said. Her voice sounded shaky to her own ears.

He held up the sheet of paper. "Do you mean it?" His voice was husky with emotion.

"I mean it," she said.

He crossed the room and stood in front of her. "Then say it."

Anna May looked into his eyes and said softly, "I love you, Ric."

She didn't know who moved first, but suddenly their lips were joined in a deeply passionate kiss.

Tenderness and desire intertwined as she pressed her body against his. It was as if saying the words to him had opened a floodgate of desire inside her. Her hands smoothed over his shoulders, and there was a muffled swish as his jacket fell to the floor. His cologne mingled with the sweet smell of jasmine, sending her senses reeling.

His hands guided the straps of her teddy off her shoulders, and within seconds the lacy creation bunched at her waist. He lifted his head and stepped out of her embrace. With gentle hands, he pushed the teddy over her hips and thighs until the silky fabric spread like a pool at her bare feet.

She could hear the raspy sound of his breathing and could see his desire for her in his brown eyes. Her world tilted as he swept her off her feet and into his arms. He carried her the short distance to the bed. Gently he laid her on the bed.

The rustle of fabric broke the silence as his shirt and pants joined his jacket on the bedroom floor. When he wore nothing, he came to the bed. With open arms, Anna May welcomed him.

A long time later, Ric held Anna May in his arms. The gentle rise and fall of her chest brushed against his side.

She loved him.

His Anna May loved him. He couldn't believe it. What had he done to deserve her love? Tightening his arms around her, he wondered how long would her love last?

"Ric," she murmured drowsily in protest.

He loosened his embrace and kissed her face. "Sorry. Go back to sleep," he whispered.

She loved him.

He wanted to believe it with all his heart. He wanted to hear her say those three words over and over again until they became a part of him. Should he trust in her love? He knew from experience that love lasted only until the other person found someone else to love. Even as the thought came to mind, he knew Anna May wasn't like his mother or grandmother. She knew him. She knew his good points and his bad points. Yet she'd remained his friend for all these years. If she loved him now, she would probably love him a few years down the road.

If he trusted her to have his child, then he could trust her to love him. His heart filled with joy as he looked at her. Her lips were slightly parted. Thick black lashes rested against her cheeks. He gently touched the chain and ring nestled between her breasts. She was so beautiful and she loved him. He kissed her face once more and whispered, "I love you, Anna May."

Ric awakened to an empty bed. Sunlight filtered through a thin opening in the curtains. He felt at peace for the first time in a long time.

His wife loved him.

He stretched and smiled in satisfaction. It felt good to be loved, he thought to himself. But he needed to tell his wife that he loved her. Ric sat up and looked at the clock on the nightstand. *No wonder I'm here alone.* Ten o'clock was late even for his wait-to-the-last-minute-to-get-out-of-bed wife.

The clank of glass tapping against glass along with the soft, muffled sound of someone climbing the stairs interrupted his thoughts and sent his heart racing with anticipation. Seconds later Anna May entered the bedroom carrying a wicker tray. Her shy smile warmed his rapidly beating heart.

"Morning, sleepyhead," she said as she walked across the room. With each step, the long, forest green robe bared a glimpse of her long legs. The robe was the same color as the teddy she'd worn the night before. He smiled as he recalled how little time she'd spent wearing the teddy.

"Morning. What's this?" he asked.

"Breakfast," she replied.

Ric raised his brows in surprise. "For me?"

"Yes, for you. Now sit up so I can put this down."

He propped his pillow on the headboard and leaned back. Anna May placed the tray across his lap. A single plate and two glasses adorned the tray. She'd prepared his favorites: cheese grits, scrambled eggs, bacon, toast with grape jelly, a tall glass of orange juice, and a glass of water.

He was humbled at her thoughtfulness. She cared enough to prepare his meal and served it to him in bed. He didn't think anyone had ever done that for him. Ric cleared his throat, but emotions made his voice husky. "Thank you, Anna May."

"You're welcome," she said then kissed his lips softly.

"Did you have breakfast already?" he asked as he picked up the fork and scooped up a helping of grits.

She walked to the other side of the bed and sat down. "Yes, I ate downstairs hours ago. I was starving. You were sleeping so peacefully, I didn't want to wake you."

He took a bite of the grits and closed his eyes. "Is there any way I can convince you to make cheese grits every weekend?"

"I don't know. It's a lot of work. Grating cheese, boiling water, standing over a hot stove," she said pondering his request. The serious expression on her face was at odds with the twinkle in her eyes.

"I understand that it's hard, back-breaking work to make cheese grits, but I think we can negotiate a deal that is satisfactory to both parties."

Anna May smiled. "And what do you suggest?"

"You make the cheese grits on the weekends, and I'll give you darn near anything you want," he replied.

"Anything?" she asked.

"Anything."

She lowered her head and looked at him from beneath her eyelashes. "Does today count?"

Ric took another bite of the grits and nodded. "Today counts."

"In that case, I know exactly what I want," she said softly.

He forgot about food when he saw her wickedly sexy smile.

From her position at his side, Anna May slid her hand down his chest and gently caressed his stomach. "You never did finish breakfast," she said lazily.

The tray with a nearly complete breakfast sat on the nightstand. "I think I was distracted." He squeezed her bare shoulder, enjoying the feel of her body next to his.

"Hmm," she answered caressing his abdomen.

"Keep that up, and I'm going to get distracted again," he said.

And he was.

* * *

"Anna May, are you asleep?" Ric's husky voice pierced the silence in their bedroom. Exhausted, they lay in a spoonlike fashion on the bed.

"Mmm."

Ric tightened his arm around her waist. "Don't fall asleep. I've got something to tell you." He would have taken a deep breath, but he was too tired. He wasn't too tired to be afraid.

"Mmm."

He put his fears aside then said, "Anna May, I love you."

He felt her body stiffen against his, then slowly she turned to face him with his arm resting on her waist.

"What?" Her voice sounded hoarse and scratchy. The look in her eyes was that of wonder and surprise.

"I said *I love you*," he replied.

She wrapped her arm around him, then caressed his side before smoothing her hand over his hip. Anna May smiled a tired smile then pinched him.

"Aw! What was that for?" he asked.

She caressed his hip, and he could see the tears in her eyes. "That's for telling me you love me when I'm too tired to do a darn thing about it."

"You don't look like you're tired and," he said pressing her hand on his hip, "you don't feel it."

He was right. All remnants of sleep had vanished when he'd spoken those three words. Slowly she caressed his hip, letting her finger glide along his waist, his shoulders, and finally his jaw. With her thumb she traced the line of his lips. "I've waited so long to hear those words from you. Say them again."

"I love you," he said then kissed her thumb.

"Again," she whispered.

Leaning forward, he kissed her lips, once, twice, over and over until she lost track of time. With each kiss, he whispered the words she longed to hear. "I love you."

The aroma of baked pork chops greeted him as he entered the kitchen. The past two weeks had been the most wonderful time of his life. It was as if admitting his love to Anna May had changed him. And it had. Warren noticed the change the following Monday and asked him what happened because he was smiling too much. He'd caught Mrs. Jones's puzzled gaze on a few occasions. Had loving his wife changed him so much? Yes, he was sure it had.

The radio played a soothing classical melody, and the dinner table was set for two. However, Anna May was missing from the room. He placed his overcoat on the back of the chair and his briefcase on the floor.

Silently she entered the room.

"Hi there, handsome. I didn't hear you come in," she said as she embraced him.

How could he have lived so long without this? he wondered and leisurely enjoyed her kiss. When he finally lifted his head, he was gasping for breath. He felt like this every time he was near her. The love and passion they shared seemed so perfect, so right. At times when he was alone, he wondered if there was some dark cloud waiting just around the corner to destroy what they'd discovered. He suppressed the thoughts, but they would surface again.

"Dinner's almost ready," she said breathlessly.

"I'll be right back," he replied then kissed her lips

again before going upstairs to the bedroom. He'd definitely changed, he thought, as he replaced his suit and tie for jeans and a sweatshirt. Before he'd married Anna May, he would have taken off only his suit jacket when he came home. In the past two weeks, eight pairs of blue jeans had appeared in the closet. Living with her had mellowed him. He spent fewer days working at home. Instead they'd fight over the remote control and watch a movie as they cuddled on the sofa. He smiled. He couldn't remember a time when they'd made it through a complete movie without finding something else to distract them. Usually each other.

She'd placed dinner on the table when he returned. They said grace and began to share the things that were happening on their jobs.

"We finally resolved the labor problem in California, so I won't have to go back anytime soon," he said.

"Good, you need a break."

"I don't know about a break. I'll be acquiring another company here in Atlanta called Wilson and Wilson. Taking it over could be just as time consuming."

"Really? Why?" she asked buttering her roll.

Ric cut his pork chop before replying. "The company's about to go bankrupt, and that's usually complicated as it is. But since it's my stepfather's . . . no, now it's my brother's firm, there're going to be some hard feelings."

"Can't you do anything to help him? What about your brother? What's going to happen to him?"

Ric felt as if she'd slapped him. Her barrage of questions and negative body language emphasized the disapproval he'd heard in her voice. "Can't I do anything to help him? This is a business deal, not a charity case," he said as put down his fork. His appetite was gone.

"But he's your brother. Surely you're going to help him," she said.

"I am helping him. As a shareholder, Adam will get a dividend at the end of the quarter when I buy the company. As it is, he wouldn't get anything. It's a good company, and with more capital it will be profitable within a year. Buying it is a good business decision."

"But it's a stinking personal decision. I would never leave either one of my brothers hanging like you're about to do to yours."

"Anna May, I don't know the man. He might as well be a stranger on the street."

"But he's not a stranger, he's family—and you don't treat family that way. Why don't you partner with him or loan him the money until he can get back on his feet? You said the company will be profitable in a year."

"Damn it, Anna May, this is business."

"No, it's not. It's family. I can't let you treat family like that."

"You don't even know the man."

"No, but I'm going to. He's a part of your family like Betty Steward is family."

He felt anger boiling up inside of him. He folded his napkin and dropped it on the table. "Let it alone, Anna May. I don't know him, and he doesn't know me. Let's leave it like that. This is my business, not yours." He rose from the table and walked upstairs to the attic. He needed to release some anger and hammering nails seemed like an excellent idea.

* * *

Anna May watched him leave the kitchen. She'd seen Ric angry before, but rarely had she seen him this angry. Well, she was angry, too. Ric had told her in no uncertain terms to butt out. She was his wife, his family. What made him think that she'd let him do something that would hurt him in the end?

With a huff, she began to clear the table. Why couldn't he see that hurting his brother's business would hurt him? He needed to resolve his relationship with his brother. If he didn't, the past would continue to be like a lock and chain around his heart, and even though he said he loved her, there would be some part of him that he would always hold back.

She wasn't about to let it happen. The sound of hammering filtered down to the kitchen. She wanted to go upstairs and talk some sense into him. Instead, she went to the telephone and called the Stewards. Betty Steward answered on the second ring.

The next day Anna May met Mrs. Steward for lunch at the 57th Fighter Group restaurant, which was adjacent to a small airport. This meeting was very important because even though they'd made up last night, Ric's past would always be like a ticking bomb waiting to explode. Ready to destroy her marriage and therefore kill all hopes of ever having a child.

The waitress led her to a table near the large window where diners could watch company planes and private jets take off and land. Betty Steward sat at the table, watching an old plane taxi down the runway. The older woman smiled. "I love watching the old planes. They have character."

Anna May sat down and watched in silence as the plane become airborne.

When they could no longer see the plane, Mrs. Steward turned from the window. "Thank you for indulging me."

"It's no problem, ma'am. Thank you for agreeing to see me so soon after your vacation. You must be tired."

"No. I'm quite rested. When John and I go on vacation, we go to rest. Resorts in Arizona are expensive in the winter, but they know how to pamper their guests. But you don't want to hear about my vacation—what can I do for you?"

Anna May waited until their server left. "I want to know about Ric's parents. What were they like? Especially his mother. Why would she leave her son with his grandmother?"

Mrs. Steward shook her head. "Pauline was a beautiful woman and she wanted beautiful things. I think she married my brother because he was in the army and was making a decent living. Pauline was poor growing up. So money was always important to her. Even in high school she was always trying to fit in with the well-to-do. When that didn't work out, she went after my brother. When they started dating, I tried to warn Trevor about her, but he was so in love with her. They were married right after high school. Then Ric came along, and Trevor was killed four years later."

She paused when their lunch arrived. "From what I understand, she met one of her old well-to-do classmates, Evan Wilson, a few years later. When she had Wilson's son, she sent Ric to live with her mother."

"But why?" Anna May asked.

"I don't know, child," she said. "But I do know

that it broke Ric's heart to leave his little brother. That grandmother of his was very vocal about him always asking to see Adam when he came to live with her. When he came to live with us, I offered to take him to see his mother and brother, but he didn't want to have anything to do with them." Mrs. Steward smiled a sad smile. "He didn't want to have anything to do with us, either."

Anna May pushed her food around on her plate. This was worse than she had thought. "I want to help Ric and Adam get to know each other, Mrs. Steward. I think he has to come to closure with his brother before he can truly love someone."

Mrs. Steward frowned. "I think you're right, but how are we going to get Ric to see it?"

Anna May shook her head. "I don't know, but I've got to think of something soon. Ric plans to let his brother's company go bankrupt then buy it. That'll probably kill any chance of getting the two brothers to get to know each other."

"You're right, that would definitely kill any relationship between them," she said then stared out the window.

"If I could loan the money to Adam, I would. Ric told me the company would be profitable in a year."

"How much money does he need?"

Anna May stated the amount.

"I could loan him the money," Mrs. Steward said softly.

"What? Mrs. Steward, that number is in the millions," Anna May said sure that she'd been misunderstood.

"I heard you, and I can loan him the money. Ric has been sending John and I money for years. We don't need it, and Ric won't take it back, so it's just sitting there.''

Stunned couldn't begin to describe the feeling she was experiencing. This sweet, grandmotherly looking woman had millions "just sitting there" as she'd put it. "So let me get this straight—you've got the money to lend, and you're willing to lend it to Adam Wilson?''

"Yes, that's right.''

Anna May stared at her in disbelief. "Mrs. Steward, you're amazing.''

"No, dear, I'm hungry.''

They ate in a comfortable silence. Anna May was worried. She knew it was right to help Adam Wilson, but she didn't look forward to telling Ric what she was doing. One thing was certain. He was going to be furious.

He'd been mad at her before, but she'd never done something that totally defied his wishes. An old saying came to mind: better to ask forgiveness than permission. She hoped Ric would be very forgiving.

Adam Wilson remained skeptical until he'd received confirmation from his banker that the electronic fund transfer had occurred. Two days ago Anna May Justice walked into his office and made him an offer he couldn't refuse. She'd arrange a loan to bail out his company, becoming his temporary partner until he paid off the loan, and in return he had to get to know his brother.

He'd thought she was joking at first. Who in their right mind would loan him money? But the way she'd talked to him about Ric made him take notice. Her love for him was plain to see, but he was still skeptical.

"The Justice Company declined my offer to partner with them. Why should you loan the money to me?"

"I'm not the Justice Company. Ric has no clue what I'm doing. I'm doing this because it's the right thing to do. I was raised to believe family always helps family. When I married Ric, you became a part of the family."

Adam smiled as he remembered the handshake that finalized the partnership. Now his company was cash-rich and he planned to expand upon that and make it the most profitable it had ever been.

"How's it going, son?" Evan Wilson said as he strolled into Adam's office.

"I'm great. Business is great. How's retirement, Dad?" he asked glancing at his father's attire. He looked like he'd just stepped off the golf course.

"Fine. Just fine. But if you need any help here, I'm available."

Adam smiled. "I don't think I'll be needing your help, Dad. My new partner has been help enough."

"Partner? Who's your partner? I never had a partner—why do you need one? I would have helped you."

Adam watched his father practically puff up with pride. He hadn't asked if the company needed the partnership. All his father was interested in was pride. "My partner prefers to remain a silent partner until the official announcement is made."

"You mean you don't want to tell your own father?"

"Nope. Now if you'll excuse me, Dad, I have a business to run."

Across the city, in an old-money neighborhood, Evan Wilson felt his blood run cold as he hung up the telephone. Adam really thought he could keep this type of information from him.

"Justice," he said in disgust. His son had partnered with Ric Justice. Cold, hate-filled rage filled him. There was no way in hell he was going to let Ric Justice have his company. He'd destroy it first. He stared out of the window and planned.

Anna May was a bundle of nerves. She had to tell Ric that she and his aunt had basically undermined his business. She couldn't put it off. It would be in the business section of tomorrow's newspaper because she'd written the press release herself.

As she paced back and forth across the kitchen floor, she prayed that Ric would understand. Eventually.

She jumped at the sound of the garage door opening. A few minutes later Ric walked inside. "Hello," she said nervously.

"Hi," he said then kissed her cheek.

"Dinner's ready whenever you are."

He rubbed his chin. "I think I'll skip dinner tonight. I'm too tired."

Skip dinner! No. Not tonight. "I've got to tell you something," she said in a panicked rush.

He raised his brows and studied her face. "Okay," he said as he sat down at the dining table.

Anna May sat opposite him with her hands on the table. She watched her hands tremble but took a deep breath. *Just tell him. Just tell him.* "Tomorrow Wilson and Wilson will make an announcement. They have a new partner."

"What?" He straightened his shoulders. Almost all

traces of fatigue had been erased. "Who partnered with Wilson and Wilson?"

Anna May stared at her hands. She felt her heart pound with apprehension.

"Anna May, who's the partner?" he demanded.

Slowly she lifted her gaze to meet his and said softly, "I am."

Rising to his feet, he glared down at her. "I don't believe this." His voice was filled with icy rage.

"I couldn't stand by and not help him. He's family."

"Family! Hell, up until a few weeks ago, you didn't know the man existed. Now he's family. I want you to call off the deal." His eyes conveyed his anger, rage, and determination.

She rose slowly, her legs nearly shaking. Anger she'd expected, not the kind of simmering rage she saw on his face. "Why? Why don't you want me to help him?"

"Just do it, Anna May. Break the partnership," his voice boomed.

"I'm not going to do it," she said with quiet dignity.

"So you've chosen Adam over me?" he asked.

"That's childish, Ric. This is about helping family, not about choosing one brother over another," she cried.

He stared at her from across the room. Slowly his expression changed from rage to an icy mask. It was as if he'd shut down his emotions. Cold and unyielding, he'd become like the Ice Man his business rivals called him. Without a word, he walked to the door.

"Where are you going, Ric? Don't leave like this." Her voice filled with anguish.

"I'll be back for my things later," he said without emotion.

"I love you, Ric."

He paused at the door for a moment then walked out.

"Men are scum. Each and every one of them," Marianne said with utter conviction.

It was Janet's turn to host the Ladies' Club. Anna May thought she would feel a little strange coming to her house as a guest. But she didn't feel anything at all. She could pinpoint the exact time she stopped feeling. It was when Ric said to her, If her actions represented love, then she could keep her love. He'd been so cold, so icy, so filled with rage when he made that statement—and she truly believed he meant every word. His actions confirmed it. He hadn't returned home in a month.

"You say that every time your ex tries to weasel out of paying child support. All men *aren't* scum," Janet said from the one end of the sofa.

"They are too scum," Marianne replied then pointed to Janet. "Didn't you just break up with your boyfriend, Miss Thang? And you"—she pointed to Raina—"isn't your boss married and trying to hit on you?"

"Yes, but—" Raina said only to be interrupted when Marianne pointed to Anna May.

"I don't even have to say what Ric is like. The no good so-and-so. I still think we should find him and beat him up."

"Marianne, you talk too much," Raina said nudging her ribs. Raina sat on the sofa between Marianne and Anna May. It was a good thing Janet sat next to Anna May because if she'd been close enough to

Marianne, Janet probably would have done more than nudge her in the ribs.

Raina had felt Anna May tense at the mention of her husband's name.

"I'd better go," Anna May said as she came to her feet.

Raina glared at Marianne.

"Don't leave, it's still early," Janet said.

"No, I'm really not good company and I want to go home."

Each of them hugged her and walked her to her car. When Anna May had driven out of view, Janet turned to Marianne. "I ought to beat your butt from now until Sunday. What were you thinking?"

Marianne held up her hands. "I wasn't thinking. I knew he was going to hurt her. We should have stopped her."

"Like we stopped you from marrying a jerk?" Raina replied.

"She doesn't look good. She's lost so much weight. I'm afraid for her," Janet said.

"I think we all are," Marianne said softly.

Evan Wilson unfolded the newspaper clipping. He scanned the article though he could recite it word for word. The paper said Anna May Justice was his son's partner, but he knew better. Ric Justice was behind the partnership. He touched the photo of Anna May Justice. She would be the first to pay, then him. Evan grinned and for the first time in a long time, he felt in control.

*   *   *

Ric stared out of the window of his office as the pale winter sun shone weakly through the clouds. The view of the Atlanta skyline went unnoticed.

He was thinking of Anna May. It seemed that's all he'd done over the last few weeks. In the beginning when he'd thought of her, he felt rage and betrayal. How could she have chosen Adam over him? When she'd partnered with his brother, he'd felt she'd chosen Adam. Like his mother had chosen Adam.

He'd left. He'd left before she could leave him, and he felt justified. But now as his anger cooled, he began to doubt his decision. The last thing she'd said to him when he walked out the door was "I love you." He had walked out on her as she cried, like his mother had walked out on him. Ric felt his heart break. The anger he'd used these few weeks to guard his heart fell away. The love that he'd refused to acknowledge burst free. He loved Anna May. That wasn't going to change, no matter what.

Did she still love him? he wondered. Could she love a man who'd turned his back on her love? A cold finger of fear rippled down his spine as he imagined living without her. There was only one way to know for sure.

Ric grabbed his coat and walked out of his office. "Mrs. Jones, cancel my appointments for the rest of the day. I'm going home."

Anna May read the instructions on the home pregnancy kit twice. The indicator was blue. Wonderfully, unmistakably blue. According to the instructions, there was a ninety-eight percent chance she was pregnant. She pressed her hand against her stomach. A child. Ric's baby was growing inside of her. It was a miracle. She said a prayer of thanksgiving. Something wonderful had come out of her ruined marriage.

She missed him so much. Not only had she lost a husband, but she'd lost her best friend. At times during the day she would reach for the telephone to call him. But what would she say to him?

It hurt so much to think that he hadn't loved her at all. How could you love someone and just turn your back on them totally? Not once had he called her. He'd come to the house to get clothes only when he knew she was at work. She'd stood in the closet and cried when she saw his suits were gone.

Maybe one day she wouldn't feel the overwhelming pain when she thought of him. Maybe the baby would give her some comfort. She walked out of the master bathroom and into the bedroom. She was pregnant. No wonder she was tired all the time. Initially she thought she was tired because she hadn't been sleeping well. Now she could barely keep her eyes open. Anna May lay on the bed and fell into a deep sleep. She didn't hear the smoke detector buzzing downstairs.

Ric turned into the driveway of his home, his heart filled with fear. Would she forgive him? Did she still love him like he loved her?

A dark sedan raced around the curve, nearly hitting him head on. Ric swerved to avoid a collision. As the car went past, he recognized his stepfather. *What was he doing here?* His scalp tingled. Something felt wrong.

He pressed down the accelerator, the Jaguar responded instantly. As he rounded the last curve, the house came into view. Yellow-orange flames danced out of the windows in the den.

Anna May.

He cut through the front lawn and came to a stop at the front door. *Don't let me be too late. Please don't let her be in the den.* His hands shook as he put the key into the front door and turned the knob. The heat had melted the candles on the table.

"Anna May!" he screamed then realized the smoke detectors drowned out his voice. He ran to the kitchen and opened the garage door. Her car was parked inside. Frantically he ran down the hall and up the stairs, the smoke burning his eyes. He could see flames through the thick smoke in the bedroom above the den when he reached the landing.

Gasping for breath he ran to the master bedroom. She lay on the bed, nearly covered in a cloud of smoke. He rushed to the bed and shook her shoulders. "Anna May! Wake up!" She didn't respond to his touch. What was wrong? Fear tore at him. She had to be all right. He couldn't lose her now.

The heat began to build inside the room. He swept her into his arms. The only way out was the way he'd come in. Flames licked the walls of the hallway. He prayed then he ran.

Anna May didn't want to wake up, but the noise wouldn't go away. Slowly she opened her eyes. Hospital. She was in the hospital. She didn't remember being sick . . . the last thing she remembered . . .

The baby. Had she lost the baby? Please, God, no. Again she heard the noise. She turned her head.

Ric sat in a chair beside the bed. His hands covered his face, and his shoulders shook. White gauze covered his shoulders, and large bandages covered his hands.

"Ric?" She tried to speak, but her throat burned like fire.

She tried to lift her hand to touch him, but it seemed to be weighted down. The noise grew louder and she realized Ric was crying.

"Ric . . ." she said his name weakly.

He lifted his head. Tears streamed down his face. "I love you, Anna May. I love you."

Epilogue

"Look, Ricky. It's a router. Wouldn't that be nice to have?" Ric said cradling his son in his arms as he slowly walked down the aisle of Home Depot.

Anna May shook her head. Who would have thought her husband would turn into the tooltime maniac—and what was worse, he was trying his best to start their six-month-old son, Garrick Trevor Jr., along the same path. While other fathers took their sons to football games, Ric took Ricky to Home Depot.

She stepped aside as another customer walked down the aisle of the do-it-yourself store and said with a smile, "He's not old enough to operate heavy machinery."

He turned and smiled sheepishly. "I know, but I want him to know what it is. Oh, look at that, Ricky—a drill press. When you're older we'll get you one like that."

Anna May laughed as she pushed the nearly full shopping cart and followed her husband and son. The two most important people in her life.

God had truly blessed her. She had a husband who loved her and a healthy, happy son. Ricky would be the only child she'd ever give birth to. A few weeks after she gave birth to Ricky, she had surgery that made it impossible for her to have other children. But they'd decided to adopt two other children in a few years.

Sometimes she had to pinch herself. Her happiness seemed to overflow. Evan Wilson was sentenced to five years in a minimum security prison on arson charges. Ric and Adam were getting to know each other and developing what she hoped was a solid, loving relationship. The Stewards were honorary grandparents to Ricky, and their relationship with Ric was rock solid. Her family thought the world of Ric. When her father called, half of the time it was to talk to Ric.

And Ric showered her with so much love, she would never doubt he loved her. Her heart filled with joy as she watched the two men in her life, her family. Ric looked up as if she'd spoken his name aloud. Their gaze met. Tenderness and love shone in his brown eyes.

Holding Ricky with one arm, he caressed her cheek with the other. "Have I told you I love you today?"

"At least four times," she said.

"Make it five. I love you, Anna May."

"I love you, too, Ric."

"Come on," he said. "Let's go home."

About the Author

Carla Fredd has lived in the Atlanta, Georgia area most of her life. Ms. Fredd is an engineer with AT&T. She is a member of Georgia Romance Writers.

She would love to hear from you. Please write to her at: PO Box 2121, Stone Mountain, Georgia 30086

Look for these upcoming Arabesque titles:

November 1996

AFTER ALL by Lynn Emery
ABANDON by Neffetiti Austin
NOW OR NEVER by Carmen Green

December 1996

EMERALD'S FIRE by Eboni Snoe
NIGHTFALL by Loure Jackson
SILVER BELLS, an Arabesque Holiday Collection

January 1997

ALL THE LOVE by Bette Ford
SENSATION by Shelby Lewis
ONLY YOU by Angela Winters